J. W. Williams

The Shell-Collector's Handbook for the Field

J. W. Williams

The Shell-Collector's Handbook for the Field

ISBN/EAN: 9783337392505

Printed in Europe, USA, Canada, Australia, Japan

Cover: Foto ©Andreas Hilbeck / pixelio.de

More available books at **www.hansebooks.com**

THE
SHELL-COLLECTOR'S
HANDBOOK
FOR THE FIELD.

J. W. WILLIAMS, M.A., D. Sc.,

Editor of " The Naturalists' Monthly."

𝔏𝔬𝔫𝔡𝔬𝔫 :

ROPER & DROWLEY; 29, LUDGATE HILL, E.C.

1888.

PREFACE.

In compiling this little Manual, I must express my indebtness to my friends, Mr. Baker Hudson, Mr. Brockton Tomlin, B.A., Miss F. M. Hele, Mr. W. Collinge, Mr. W. Nelson, and Mr. J. W. Taylor, the Editor of "The Journal of Conchology," for supplying me with much valuable information and help. To the works and papers of Gwyn Jeffreys, Alfred Moquin-Tandon, Baudon, Carl Agardh Westerlund, O. Boettger, Colbeau, Fischer, Ralph Tate, Macalister, Huxley, Gegenbaur, Balfour, Rymer Jones, Milnes Marshall, Ashford, Ralph Tate, Woodward, E. Von Martens, Rimmer, Roebuck, Nelson, Simroth, Taylor, Adams, Emil Adolf Rossmassler, Lessona and Pollonera, Gray, Turton, Catlow, Locard, Picard, Pascal, Dumont, Mortillet, and Cockerell, I must also express my obligations.

The varieties described include those which have been verified by the Council of the Conchological Society or by myself; and any deviation from the typical form found by the collector not mentioned in this volume should be sent to the Referee Council of the Conchological Society, Leeds, for verification.

J. W. W.

51, PARK VILLAGE EAST, N.W.

INDEX.

CHAPTER I.

THE ANATOMY OF A SNAIL.

THE

SHELL COLLECTOR'S HANDBOOK FOR THE FIELD.

CHAPTER I.

THE ANATOMY OF A SNAIL.

THE SHELL.—The shell of a Gasteropod is a cone with the apex more or less oblique. It may be globose, auriculate, oval, ovoidal, lenticular, pyriform, ulate, pyramidal, lanceolate, discoid, trochoid, turbinated, auriculate or turretted. Generally it is coiled round a central axis or *columella*, each coil being a *whorl*, and the shell being then *uni-* or *multi-whorled*. The columella sometimes opens to the exterior by a foramen (*umbilicus*) which may be closed by a shelly deposit or *umbilical callus*. The line of junction between successive whorls is the *suture*, and the apex, or oldest part of the shell, the *nucleus*. The last whorl has the name of *body whorl*, and that portion of it which overlaps the columella is known as the `columellar lobe` The aperture of the body whorl is shaped according to the contour of the mantle edge, and is surrounded by a lip or *peritreme*. It may be entire as in the phytophagous species, or prolonged into siphons as in the carnivorous species.

If the spiral of the shell be turned to the left with the mouth towards the right, the shell is said to be *sinistral* or *laötrope*, and if to the right with the mouth to the left *dextral* or *dexiotrope*. Each successive growth of the shell is represented by lines— *lines of growth*—arranged concentrically with the nucleus. In the Limacidæ the shell is rudimentary, and situated under the mantle.

The colour of the shell exists entirely in the *periostracum* or *epidermis*, and Camerano (Richerche intorno alla distribuzione dei colori nel regno animale. Mem. Acc. Tor. xxxvi. pp. 329, 360), finds that of all colours black is rare ; brown, grey, yellow, white and red common ; violet relatively abundant ; blue not rare, and green infrequent.

Beneath the epidermis is a densely calcified layer (*honeycomb layer*), showing a confused striated superficial portion, and a deeper portion of vertical prisms. Below this again is the *nacreous* or *mother of pearl layer*, consisting of thickly calcified laminæ placed upon one another, with the axes of the plates, in successive layers, set at right angles.

In some species the aperture of the shell is closed normally by a horny or shelly plate (*operculum*) which differs from the true shell in having more conchiolin entering into its composition. In non-operculated land shells, during the winter months the mouth is closed by a layer of mucus impregnated with calcareous salts (*epiphragm, hypophragm, hybernaculum* or *clausilium*) which has recently been shown by a German observer to be a secretion of the liver-cells.

THE BODY.—The body is usually divided into two portions—the one (*prostoma*) including all in front of the mantle edge, the other (*metastoma*) all behind it. That portion of the body habitually contained within the shell is often spoken of as the *visceral hump*. This visceral hump is covered by a tent or roof, extremely vascular in character, called the *mantle*, a portion of which is visible externally just below the peritreme (*collar*).

The body external to the shell presents ten points for examination, best seen when the animal is extended. In front is a rounded extremity—the *head*—bearing on its dorsal surface two *posterior* or *dorsal tentacles*, and two *anterior* or *ventral tentacles*, and on its lower or ventral surface the *mouth* bounded by two lateral lips and one inferior lip. The dorsal tentacles are the longer, and bear at their extremities the eyes. Both pairs of tentacles can be inverted into the body at the will of the animal. The *foot* is the large muscular expansion on the lower surface of the prostoma, and by means of it the animal walks. Below the mouth is the *aperture of the pedal gland*. Behind the right lip, and just below the right dorsal tentacle, the *genital aperture* exists. And in the collar on the right side is a large round foramen—the *pulmonary or respiratory orifice*—and closely associated with this, a smaller aperture obtains, which is the termination of the *duct of the renal organ*. Below and to the right

of the pulmonary aperture, the *anus*, or *vent*, is
placed, appearing as a slit-like hole.

THE DIGESTIVE SYSTEM.—The mouth leads back
into the *buccal mass*, or *pharynx*, a reddish muscular
cavity, containing two or four true cartilaginous plates,
which form an early example of an endoskeleton.
(Macalister).   On the floor of the pharynx is an up-
growth of connective and muscular tissue, overlying
which, is a chitinous sheet beset with teeth which
point backwards.   The whole of this apparatus is
termed the *odontophore*, and the chitinous plate, with
its teeth, the *radula*, or *lingual ribbon*.   The odontophore is supported by a pair of cartilaginous plates,
to the anterior and posterior surfaces of which muscles
are attached, so that the radula may perform, by their
alternate contraction and relaxation, a backward and
forward motion.   The radula is then a rasping organ,
and bites against one of the cartilaginous plates, which
we have previously mentioned as existing in the
buccal mass.   In the Pulmonata, this plate, or jaw, is
vertical, and placed on the upper pharyngeal wall;
but according to Macalister, in Paludina, there are
opposed lateral jaws armed with flat plates, that are
situated in a horizontal direction.   The teeth are
usually strengthened by a siliceous deposit, and, when
worn away, are replaced by the development of some
others from behind.

The radula consists of a central or axial plate
(*rachidian teeth, rachis teeth, dentes*) and a lateral plate
on each side (*uncini*).   The method of the formula
for describing the numbers and position of these
teeth, is as follows:—" The central teeth of the

rachidian series are denominated by the sign 1 when present, and 0 when absent ; the admedian teeth by the signs 1, 2, 3 . . . . according to the number present ; while the lateral teeth are noted by the sign 0, repeated as often as there are lateral teeth on either side ; when the number of admedian or of lateral teeth is very large, the sign x is used in place of 1, 2, 3 . . . . or 0 repeated. For example, when, as in Æolis, there are no lateral teeth, we write the formula 0. 1. 0 ; that of Amphisphyra, is 1. 1. 1 ; that of Aplysia, 13. 1. 13 ; and that of Onicidium, 54. 1. 54." (Jeffrey Bell. Comp. Anat. p. 136). In some of the Helices, the teeth may reach the enormous number of 39,596. The manner of the working of the radula may easily be observed by watching a *Limnæa stagnalis* cleaning the confervæ from the glass side of an aquarium.

The buccal mass passes back by a thin-walled *œsophagus* into a spindle-shaped cavity, the *crop*, which lies in that part of the visceral hump situated in the body whorl, and at the sides of which two large white *salivary glands** open by means of their ducts, one on each side. Following the alimentary canal still on, we next come to a slightly dilated portion of it, which is known as the *stomach*, and which lies near the commencement of the second turn of spiral, close to the surface of the visceral hump. Then leaving this, we arrive at the commencement of

---

* Recent researches show that this salivary gland contains free sulphuric and free hydrochloric acid, and that there can be but little doubt it has an amylolytic function in converting starch into sugar.

the intestine, which makes a S-shaped turn through the *digestive gland*, and then passes into the *rectum*, which runs along the right side of the mantle cavity to the anus. This *digestive gland* has two lobes—a right and a left. The right lobe lies in the upper half of the body whorl, and is divided into three lobes, each lobe possessing a duct of its own. These ducts, however, unite into a common duct before emptying themselves into the right side of the stomach. The left lobe is situated in the upper turns of the spiral. It has one duct which opens on the left side of the stomach, nearly opposite the common duct of the right lobe. Three kinds of cells have been demonstrated as existing in this so-called liver, or digestive gland. One set becomes black on treatment with osmic acid (*ferment cells*); another contains calcic phosphate and calcic carbonate, and is concerned in the function of producing the epiphragm (*calcareous* or *calciferous cells*); while the other set (*hepatic cells*) excrete yellowish-looking globules, which are passed away with the fæces, and which, in my thinking, serve the same function in the snail's economy, as the bile in the human body.

The Circulating System.—The *pericardium* is oval, about an inch in length in the largest species, and placed to the left of the kidney, and in the roof of the mantle cavity. It is in communication with the kidney by a canal—the *reno-pericardial canal*.

The *heart* consists of a thin-walled *auricle* and a thick-walled *ventricle*, separated from each other by an *auriculo-ventricular valve*. From the front end of the ventricle the *aorta* arises, and immediately divides

into two branches, one taking its course to the apex
of the spire, and supplying the liver, intestine, and
reproductive organs (*posterior aorta*); while the other
(*anterior aorta*) runs forward, gives branches to the
salivary glands, head, tentacles, and body-wall, and a
large branch—*the pedal artery*—which passes backwards along the foot to supply it. There are no
capillaries, and the arteries end by funnel-shaped
openings in the lacunæ of the interstices of the
tissues. From these lacunæ the blood passes into the
various sinuses of the body. Two of these sinuses
run along the sides of the foot (*pedal sinuses*), one on
either side, and another (*visceral sinus*) courses from
the apex of the shell-cavity to the posterior end of the
mantle-cavity, ending in a circular *pulmonary sinus*.
From this pulmonary sinus efferent vessels carry the
blood to the roof of the mantle-cavity to be aërated,
and then coverge to form a *pulmonary vein*, which
runs in a straight line along the roof of the respiratory chamber back to the auricle, previously
receiving the *renal vein* from the kidney. The pedal
sinuses do not seem to be in direct communication
with the pulmonary sinus, and any blood passing from
one to the other must be transmitted by way of the
lacunæ. According to the researches of Harless and
Wicke, in the majority of the Pulmonata, the blood is
bluish and richly corpusculated; in others, whitish and
opaline; while in the Genus Planorbis, it is red in
colour.

THE RESPIRATORY ORGANS.—In the Branchio-
gasteropoda—where the organs are so formed as to
breathe air dissolved in the watery medium in which

they live—the respiratory organs consist of pectinated
branchiæ enclosed in a branchial chamber formed by
a folding-in of the mantle, the water being admitted,
in many species, by a tubular prolongation of the
mantle edge (*anterior siphon*), and expelled through a
similarly constructed *posterior siphon*. But in the
Pulmogasteropoda—which inspire atmospheric air—
inspiration and expiration are effected through the
pulmonary aperture. This pulmonary aperture leads
into the mantle-cavity (lung), the upper and lateral
walls of which are formed by a thin fold of the body-
skin (*mantle*), and the floor by the convex, muscular
dorsal wall of the body. The mantle is extremely
vascular in character, the vascularity being due to the
reticulated arrangement of the afferent and efferent
pulmonary vessels which converge to form the pulmonary vein. There the blood is arterialised, by the
absorption of oxygen from the air, and the excretion
of carbonic dioxide as a waste tissue product.*

Inspiration is effected by the contraction of the
muscular bulging on the floor of the mantle-cavity.
This produces a flattening of the floor, and, consequently, an enlargement of the cavity, and air rushes
in through the pulmonary orifice to fill up the void.

The return of the muscles to their former state of
relaxation results in an expiration. An analogous condition may be found in the contraction and relaxation
of the mammalian diaphragm.

THE KIDNEY, FOOT-GLAND, AND TAIL-GLAND.—The

---

* Paludina has both branchiæ and lung, while Limnæa
possesses no branchiæ, and uses its air receptacle as a hydrostatic
organ.

kidney in the Pulmonata is situated between the pulmonary vein and the heart, and communicates with the pericardial cavity by the reno-pericardial canal. It consists of two parts, one thin-walled and saccular, the other yellowish and of a lamellated structure. It corresponds with the *Organ of Bojanus* of the Bivalves.

The duct of the kidney or *ureter* commences in its posterior portion, runs alongside of, but dorsad, to the rectum, and opens into the mantle-cavity near to the anus.

The foot-gland or pedal gland is a tubular sac, lined with ciliated epithelium, which runs the length of the foot, and opens to the exterior just below the mouth. A similar tail-gland obtains in the genera Geomalcus and Arion.

THE NERVOUS SYSTEM.—Lying over the œsophagus are a pair of pear-shaped masses of nervous tissue— the *supraœsophageal* or *cerebral ganglia*—from which arise nerves which pass to the tentacles and lips, and a large pair of nerves—the *buccal nerves*—which course by the side of the œsophagus, to end in two buccal ganglia placed externally to the ducts of the salivary glands. These buccal ganglia are united by a commissure from which arise nerves to supply the buccal mass.

Below the œsophagus are two closely approximated ganglia—the *subœsophageal ganglia*—formed of an anterior portion (*pedal ganglia*) which is divided from the posterior portion (*viscero-pleural ganglia*) by the passage of the aorta through the centre of the mass. The pedal ganglia innervate the foot, while from the viscero-pleural ganglia nerves pass to the viscera and the body-wall (*pallial nerves*). The supra- and sub-œsophageal ganglia are spoken of collectively as the *nerve collar.*

The supra- and sub-œsophageal ganglia communicate with each other by a pair of connectives, and between these the *auditory nerve* courses to the auditory organ.

A microscopic examination of a ganglion shows it to consist of unipolar, sometimes bipolar, nerve cells, imbedded in a matrix of neurilemma, which in the *Zonites* is said to contain unstriped muscle fibres.

THE AUDITORY ORGANS.—The auditory organs (*otocysts*) are a pair of small rounded sacs, situated either in the substance of the pedal ganglia or in close relation with them ; and in the genus Paludina are moveable by muscles. Each contains in its interior a large number of calcareous granules (*otoliths*), which strike upon the terminal filaments of the auditory nerve, and thus communicate a wave of change to the supra-œsophageal ganglia. In some Pulmonata the otocyst is in communication by a canal with the external world.

THE EYES.—The eyes are carried on the distal ends of the posterior tentacles, and, from this reason, this pair of tentacles has been called the *ommatophores.* They are simple in character, globular or oval in contour, and can be regenerated, if destroyed, by the animal. Accommodation for long distances seems to be defective, for snails cannot distinguish objects till they are within a quarter of an inch from the eyes. Each eye consists of a cornea, lens, and strongly pigmented retina, and leads back by an optic nerve – which when the tentacle is invaginated into the body is coiled up in a beautiful fashion—to the nerve to the tentacle, of which it forms a branch.

THE OLFACTORY ORGANS.—Most probably the olfactory organ is the pedal gland which has already been described. Still there are authors who localise the sense of smell in the anterior tentacles, or in the lobate processes surrounding the mouth.

THE REPRODUCTIVE ORGANS.—The Opisthobranchiata and Pulmonata are monœcious with the exception, perhaps, of *Limax lævis*, which, according to the recent researches of Simroth, has the sexes distinct (*vide* S. B. Ges. Leipsig, 1883, p. 74). The principal reproductive organ is the *hermaphrodite gland* or *ovotestis*, a yellowish gland situated in the left lobe of the digestive gland, and near the inner side of the second whorl. This combines the functions of ovary and testis, and although the cells composing it are microscopically alike, yet the regions where the ova and spermatozoa are developed are distinct and well defined from one another. Histologically the ovotestis consists of digitate follicles, in each of which the ova are developed on the outer wall, and the spermatozoa in the more central portions. Lodged in the right lobe of the digestive gland is a yellowish-white tongue-shaped organ—*the albumen gland*—from which a duct arises which unites in some portion of its extent with another duct from the hermaphrodite gland—the *hermaphrodite duct*—forming a common duct which at length divides into two—one, the longer, called the *vas deferens*, and the other the *oviduct*.

The vas deferens belongs to the male portion of the generative organs, the oviduct to the female portion. We will take these separately.

The vas deferens runs along the side of the female organs, under the retractor muscle of the tentacle, and terminates in the *penis sac.* Before its termination, a diverticulum is given off as the *flagellum,* in which the spermatozoa become, as it were, glued together to form the *spermatophore.*

The penis sac is the continuation of the vas deferens, and opens to the exterior at the genital aperture, a little below and behind the right dorsal tentacle. This tube contains a conical intromittent organ (*penis*), and may be everted, at the pleasure of the animal, by contracting the retractor muscle which has its origin from the floor of the mantle-cavity and its insertion into the penis sac just above the penis.

The female reproductive organs are none the less complicated. Like the vas deferens the oviduct has a diverticulum, which, in this case, is called the *receptaculum seminis* or *spermatheca,* and serves to lodge a spermatophore received from another snail. In some snails this receptaculum seminis is single, and consists of not more than one diverticulum. But in the majority of species—and notably in *Helix aspersa*—there is another diverticulum, which becomes dilated at its cæcal extremity, and ends near the division of the aorta. Below this point the oviduct may be spoken of as the *vagina.* The vagina ends in the penis sac, thus producing a common gential canal or *vestibule.* Into the vagina opens the two ducts of the tufted *muciparous glands,* and just above or below these openings is a large pear-shaped sac—the *dart sac*—which contains a calcareous spicule called the *spiculum amoris* or *dart*. The shape of the dart varies in different species, and the reader wishing to learn more about its various modifications may consult the papers of Mr. Ashford, in the past numbers of the " Journal of Conchology." But what function these darts may serve is an unsettled question. It is, however, a certain matter, that before two snails engage in *coitus* they discharge their darts at each other, and that the one strives to evade the dart of the other. Possibly they are used as an amorous greeting. But my friend, Mr. W. Collinge, in a paper on " The Darts of the Helicidæ," which he read before the Leeds Naturalists' Club and Scientific Association, on October 24th, 1887, considers them as degenerate weapons of defence, which, in former ages, were probably much stronger and oftener used—and doubtless he may, in some measure, be correct.

During coition, one snail exchanges its spermatophore with the other, and these become lodged in the receptaculum seminis of each other, where they break up again into spermatozoa, and fertilise the ova as they are coming down the oviduct.

The eggs are laid in a string, which is called the *nidamental ribbon,* or enclosed in horny capsules.

LITERATURE (TO WHICH THE READER MAY ADVAN-
TAGEOUSLY REFER):

Balfour.   "Comparative Embryology."
                          Vol. I. 1885.
Bell (Jeffrey).   "Comparative Anatomy and
                          Physiology." 1885.
Binney.   Terrestial Air-Breathing Mol-
                          lusca of the United
                          States. 1851-57.
Blockmann.   " Ueber die Entwicklung der
                          Neritina fluviatilis." *Zeit.*
                          für. wiss. Zool., xxxvi.
                          1881.
      "   " Beiträge zur Kenntnis der
                          Entwicklung der Gastero-
                          poden." *Ibid.,* xxxviii.
                          1883.
Bobretsky.   " Studien über die embryonale
                          Entwicklung der Gastero-
                          poden." *Arch. f. Mikr.*
                          Anat., xiii. 1879.
Bronn and Keferstein. " Malacozoa."   In   Bronn's
                          Klassen und Ordnungen
                          der Their-Reichs. 1862-
                          66.
Bütschli.   " Entwicklungsgeschichtliche
                          Beiträge (Paludina vivi-
                          para)." *Zeit. f. wiss.*
                          Zool. xxix. 1877.

Clarapède.	" Anatomie u. Entwickl. der Neritina fluviatilis." Muller's *Archiv.* 1857.]
Claus and Sedgwick.	" Elementary Text-book of Zoology." Vol. ii. 1885.
Cuvier.	" Mémoirs pour servier à l'histoire et à l'anatomie des Mollusques." 1816.
Eisig.	" Beitr. z. Anat. u. Entwickl. der Geschlechtsorg. von Lymnæus." *Zeitschr f. wiss. Zool.*, vol. xix. 1869.
Fol.	" Sur le développement des Gastéropodes pulmonés." *Compt. rend.*, 1875, pp. 523-536.
Gegenbaur.	" Comparative Anatomy." English translation. 1878.
,,	" Beit. z. Entwicklungsgesch. der. Landgasteropoden." *Zeit. f. wiss. Zool.* Vol. III. 1851.
Haddon.	" An Introduction to the Study of Embryology." 1887.
,,	" Notes on the Development of Mollusca." *Quart. Journ. Micr. Sci.*, xxii. 1882.
Huxley.	" The Anatomy of Invertebrated Animals." 1877.

c

Jhering. " Entwicklungsgeschichte von Helix. *Jenaische Zeitschrift.* Vol. IX. 1875.

Jourdain. " Sur le Développement du Tube digestif des Limaciens." *Compt. Rend.* xcviii. 1884.

Lankester. Art. " Mollusca." *Ency. Brittanica* (ix.), xvi. 1883.

,, " On the Development of the Pond-snail." *Quart. Journ. Micr. Sci.* Vol. xiv. 1874.

,, " On the Coincidence of the Blastophore and Anus in Paludina vivipara." *Ibid.* Vol. xvi. 1876.

Leydig. " Ueber Paludina vivipara." *Zeit. f. wiss. Zool.* Vol. II. 1850.

Macalister. " Introduction to Animal Morphology." 1876.

Mark. " Maturation, Fecundation, and Segmentation of Limax Campestris." *Bull. Mus. Comp. Zool.* Harvard. 1881.

Marshall and Hurst. " Practical Zoology." 1887.

Meuron " Sur les Organs renaux des Embryons d'Helix." *Compt. Rend.,* xcviii. 1884.

M'Murrich.	" On the Existence of a Post-oral Band of Cilia in Gasteropod Veligers." *John Hopkins' Univ. Circ., Baltimore,* v. 1885.
,,	" A contribution to the Embryology of the Prosobranch Gasteropods." *Studies Biol. Lab. John Hopkins' Univ., Baltimore,* iii. 1886.
Nicholson.	" Manual of Zoology." Seventh edition. 1887.
Patten.	" Eyes of Molluscs and Arthropods." *Mittheil. Zool. Neapel.,* vi. 1886.
Pfeiffer.	" Monographia pneumonopomorum viventium." 1852. Supplement, 1858.
Rabl.	" Die Ontogenie d. Süsswasser-Pulmonaten," *Jenaische Zeitschrift,* Vol. v. 1879,
,,	" Bietz. zur. Entwicklungsgesch der Prosobranchier." *Sitzungsber. Akad. Wien.,* lxxxvii. 1883.
,,	" Ueb. d. Entwick. d. Tellerschnecke (Planorbis)." *Morph. Jahr.* Vol. v. 1869.

Schmidt.	" Ueb. Entwick. von Limax agrestis." Muller's *Archiv.* 1851.
Warneck.	" Ueb. d. Bild. u. Entwick. d. Embryos bei Gasteropoden." *Bullet. Soc, natural de Moscou.* t. xxiii. 1850.
Zeigler.	" Die Entwicklung von Cyclas cornea. Lam. (Sphærium corneum, L)." *Zeit. für. wiss. Zool.,* xli. 1885.

CHAPTER II.

THE ANATOMY OF A FRESH-WATER MUSSEL.

CHAPTER II.

THE ANATOMY OF A FRESH-WATER MUSSEL.

THE SHELL.—The shell of a Lamellibranch—for that is the class to which the Fresh-water Mussel belongs—is a bivalve. The valves are united to one another by an elastic *ligament*, and near to this ligament is a rounded blunt prominence of the shell known as the *umbo*. The external surface of the shell is marked by lines—*lines of growth*—running concentric to the umbo. The interior of each valve is white and iridescent, and near to its dorsal border are two depressions which mark the insertion of the anterior and posterior adductor muscles, called respectively the *anterior* and *posterior adductor impressions*. Joining these two impressions a faint line can be observed—the *pallial line*—indicating the attachment of the pallial muscle of the mantle. Continuous with the posterior border of the anterior adductor impression is another depression—the *anterior retractor impression*—and near to it a distinct fourth impression will be noticed—the *protractor impression*. The *posterior retractor impression* is continuous with the anterior portion of the posterior adductor impression. At the dorsal margin the valves are united together along a line, which is known as the *hinge-line.* Near to this line, in some species as *Sphærium corneum,* there are teeth which fit into corresponding hollows in the opposite valve. Those directly under the umbo are called *cardinal teeth,* those on either side *lateral teeth.* The length of the shell is measured from its anterior to its posterior margin, and the breadth from its dorsal to its ventral margin.

Microscopical examination of the shell shows three layers, the *periostracum* or *outer layer,* the *prismatic* or *middle layer,* and the *nacreous* or *inner layer.* The periostracum is thin and horny; the prismatic layer is composed of polygonal prisms placed side by side in a pallisade manner, and the nacreous layer consists of super-imposed calcareous laminæ.

Muscular System.—The *anterior* and *posterior adductors* run from one valve of the shell to the other. The *anterior* and *posterior retractors of the foot* are situated near these, and pass from their origins to their insertion into the foot. The *protractor muscle* arises from the protractor impression, and spreads out in a fan-shaped manner over the upper part of the foot. Several small muscles—the *pallial muscles*—attach the mantle to the pallial line, while some muscles resembling these, and known as the *lesser retractors,* arise in front of the umbo, and spread over the surface of the digestive gland.

The Mantle and Mantle-Cavity.—The mantle is divided into two lobes, a right and a left, which are continuous with each other on the dorsal side of the animal. Between the two lobes is the mantle- or pallial-cavity containing the gills, foot, labial palps, and the greater portion of the visceral mass. It is divided into two chambers by the base of the gills, one larger and more ventral taking the name of the *branchial chamber*; the other, the smaller and more dorsal, the name of the *supra-branchial chamber*. The hinder of the supra-branchial chamber forms the *cloacal chamber*.

The foot protrudes through the anterior end of the cleft between the mantle-lobes, and the inhalent and exhalent siphons protrude through the posterior end. The inhalent will be distinguished from the exhalent aperture by possessing tentacular fringes. A current of water sets in through the inhalent aperture, circulates through the pallial chamber, and returns by the exhalent aperture, bearing with it the excretory products of the body.

THE ALIMENTARY SYSTEM.—The mouth is situated between the anterior adductor and the anterior border of the foot. It is bounded by two triangular processes—the *labial palps*—and passes back by a short and straight œsophagus into a dilated chamber, or *stomach*, which lies in the substance of the digestive gland, the duct of which opens into it near its anterior end. The intestine takes a convoluted course, becomes into intimate relation with the generative gland, pierces the anterior end of the pericardium, and running back horizontally as a straight tube (*rectum*) passes through the ventricle of the heart and finally ends by an opening—the *anus*—on the dorsal side of the cloacal chamber.

The rectum has a well-marked infolding of its inner wall—the *typhosole*—the function of which seems to be the production of a larger absorptive surface.

The liver or digestive gland lies on the sides of the stomach, into which it opens by several bile ducts. It is multi-lobed, and of a brownish colour.

THE GILLS.—The gills lie between the visceral mass and the mantle. Each gill consists of a pair of lamellæ, and each lamella is composed of a large number of gill filaments which have become fused together so as to form a perforated trellis-work-like structure. The blood circulates through these gill filaments, which thus form a kind of ciliated grating through and over which the water is driven.

THE CIRCULATORY ORGANS.—The heart consists of two lateral auricles and one median ventricle, and is situated just under the hinge-line and above and behind the digestive gland. The pericardial cavity is pierced by the intestine.

From the anterior end of the ventricle the *anterior aorta* arises, and after entering the visceral mass divides into *visceral* and *pedal arteries*, which supply the anterior two-thirds of the body, including the foot, labial palps, anterior part of the mantle, and intestine. From the posterior end of the ventricle, the *posterior aorta* arises, and, after dividing into a right and a left branch, supplies the remaining portion of the body.

These vessels, as in the Gasteropods, break up into lacunar spaces, from whence the blood, after giving nutriment to the tissues, finds its way into a large sinus situated under the pericardium, and known as the *vena cava*. From this it is carried to the organ of Bojanus, and thence by the *afferent branchial veins* to the gills, where it becomes purified, losing carbonic anhydride, and gaining oxygen.

From the gills it is returned by the *efferent branchial veins* to the auricles. A plexus of vessels, known as the *organ of Keber*, exists near where the efferent branchial veins open into the auricles; but its function has not yet been demonstrated. The blood from the mantle-lobes is returned direct to the heart, and does not circulate either through the Organs of Bojanus, or the gills.

THE ORGANS OF BOJANUS.—The Organs of Bojanus or the kidneys are two in number, and situated just beneath the pericardium. Each will be found, on examination, to consist of a glandular, and a non-glandular part. The glandular portion communicates anteriorily with the pericardial cavity, and posteriorly with the non-glandular part or *vestibule*, from whence the excretory products are conducted to the exterior by a thin walled *ureter*, which opens by the external renal aperture between the two lamellæ of the inner gill, and just posterior to the external opening of the generative gland. Urea and uric acid have been recently demonstrated in these organs, and they serve, therefore, an excretory function, and correspond to the kidneys of the higher animals.

THE NERVOUS SYSTEM.—The nervous system consists of three pairs of ganglia—the *cerebral, pedal,* and the *osphradial* or *parieto-splanchnic ganglia.* The cerebral ganglia are situated one on each side of the mouth, and give off labial, pallial, muscular, and anterior branchial branches. They correspond to the supraœsophageal ganglia of the snail, and are united by a commissure which runs in the middle line over the mouth. From these ganglia two connectives arise, the *cerebro-pedal connectives*, which unite the cerebral ganglia with another pair of ganglia which are orange-coloured, and situated in the foot, known as the *pedal ganglia.*

From the cerebral ganglia also proceed another pair of connectives—the *cerebro-osphradial connectives*—to the *osphradial* or *parieto-splanchnic ganglia,* which are placed under the posterior adductor muscle, giving branches to the mantle and to the substance of this muscle. The pedal ganglia give branches to the foot and the auditory organs.

THE AUDITORY ORGAN.—The auditory organ or *otocyst* consists of a small rounded or oval sac filled with fluid, and containing a central otolith. The auditory nerve is a branch of the pedal ganglion.

THE OSPHRADIUM.—An organ in close relation with the osphradial ganglion, and which consists of a layer of elongated epithelium, has been called the *osphradium* by Lankester, and is believed to be olfactory in function.

THE REPRODUCTIVE ORGANS.—Unlike the Gastero-pods the Lamellibranchs are diœcious. The generative glands are macroscopically alike in both sexes, and it is only on a microscopical examination that the testis may be distinguished, by its spermatozoa, from the ovary, with its ova. They are racemose in character, and occupy a large portion of the upper part of the foot. Their contents escape into the surrounding water through the genital aperture which opens on the exterior of the body just below the orifice of the ureter. In the female, however, the ova do not pass directly out of the body, but congregate in large numbers between the two lamellæ of the outer gill where they develop into peculiar larval forms—which at one time were considered parasites of the mussel—known as *Glochidia.* Each valve of a Glochidium-shell is shaped like an equilaterial triangle, with the apex incurved and produced into a sharp saw-edged tooth. A single adductor muscle is present ; the foot is small and slightly developed, and in its place two filaments—the *byssal filaments*—are seen projecting from the larva.

In this form the embryo is ejected from the gill of its brood-mother into the water. Then sinking down to the bottom of the pond the shell gapes widely, for the single adductor muscle is not strong enough to keep the valves together. Swimming by the flapping of its valves, when it becomes a little more developed, the young Anodon attaches itself by means of its byssal filaments to either the gill-covers, lips, or fins of a fish—especially Leuciscus and Gobio—and fixes its sharp teeth into its body. Remaining for a time in this parasitic condition, the single adductor muscle and the byssal threads atrophy, and in their place the anterior and posterior adductors become developed, and the foot more developed. Changes go on until the larva has become like the parent from which it originated, and then the young Anodon loses its hold, drops down into the bottom of the water in which it exists, and commences the every-day life of its mother.

KEFERSTEIN'S ANALOGY.—Keferstein has compared

a Lamellibranch to a book whose back is represented by
the hinge-line, its cover by the valves, its fly-leaves
by the mantle-lobes, its second and third pages at
each side by the gill lamellæ, and its interior by the
visceral mass and foot. The aptness of this compari-
son will now be very readily conceived by the reader.

LITERATURE.

(In this list the general text-books noticed on pages
      16 to 20 have not been included.) ‑

Bojanus.   " Ueber die Anthem-und Kreislaufwerk,
            zenge der zweischaligen Muscheln."
            Isis, 1819, 1820, 1827.

Braun.   " Postembryonale Entwicklung. d. Süss-
            wasser Muscheln." *Zoologischer Garten.*

Davaine.   " Sur le génération des Huîtres." Paris,
            1853.

Deshayes. " Art. Conchifera," in Todd's Encyclo-
            pædia, Vol. I., 1836.

Garner.   " On the Anatomy of the Lamelli-
            branchiate Conchifera." *Trans. Zool.
            Soc.,* London, Vol. II., 1841.

Leydig.   " Ueber Cyclas cornea." Müller's *Archiv,*
            1855.

Lovén.   " Bidrag til Känned. om Utweckl. af Moll.
            Acephala Lammellibr." *Kongl. Veten-
            skaps-Akad. Handl.,* Stockholm,
            1848-1850.

Schmidt.   " Ueb. d. Entwick. von Cyclas calyculata."
            Müller's *Archiv,* 1854.

Stepanoff. " Ueb. die Geschlechtsorgane u. die Ent-
            wicklung von Cyclas," *Archiv f.
            Naturgeschichte,* 1865.

ON COLLECTING AND PRESERVING LAND & FRESH-WATER SHELLS.

CHAPTER III.

COLLECTING AND PRESERVING LAND AND FRESH-WATER SHELLS.

I MAY lay down five golden rules which must never be forgotten by the shell-collector when out on a field-excursion. They are these :—

1. Never leave a stone unturned.

2. Never pass by a nettle without a full examination of its stem, branches, leaves, and the vegetation which grows below and around it.

3. Never leave untouched, and unexamined, moss at the roots of trees, or the dead leaves under them.

4. Always examine the vegetation on walls, and the grass which grows around their foundations.

5. Never forget when searching for water-specimens to examine the water plants, and the under surface of any floating log of wood as well as the bed of the pond, brook, or stream.

These are *rules*, but, in addition, I would say examine everywhere, for there is scarcely any portion of the earth's surface that will not discover specimens to an observant eye.

The apparatus required to collect land-shells and slugs consists of simply your own nimble fingers, a sharp, observant eye, and a few chip or match-boxes for carrying your specimens home.

D

Water-shells, on the other hand, will have to be obtained partly with your fingers, and partly with a water-net and dredge. Water-weeds, brought to the bank by means of a stick, can be examined with the hand at the time, or taken home in bags for examination at an early leisure. The net will be serviceable in sweeping the surface of the pond for any floating specimens, and for the detachment of any shells which may be attached to the water-plants that are too firmly rooted to allow the collector to drag them to the shore with his stick. The net I generally use is made of strong book-muslin, of an oblong bag-shape, attached to a galvanized iron-ring, which is inserted into a long, but withal wieldable, handle.

The dredge is useful for making an examination of the bed of the pond or river for Unios and Anodons in particular. It may be obtained from any seller of natural-history wares, or made by the collector himself. The best form of this apparatus is the one with a square iron frame, having a small-meshed net behind, and from the four angles of which ropes are attached in such a manner that, at some distance from the dredge, they all end equally at one point, from which point a single rope extends to the hand of the collector. The dredge should be so weighted as to enable it to slide along the bed of the pond without tilting over its contents.

When you have arrived at your home after a day's collecting, the shells obtained should be instantly— and on that day—killed by means of boiling water, and the animals extracted. In the case of univalves, this extraction is made by the employment of bent needles stuck head first into handles. The animals of the larger specimens will come out easily this way; but those of the smaller ones sometimes break inside. To obviate this difficulty, these last should be killed in boiling water, to which some salt has been added. This renders their extraction much easier.

The confervoid growth often found on the shells of water-snails should be removed by means of a tooth-brush, dipped in pure water, with plenty of elbow-grease. Should, however, pure water fail for this purpose, a *very weak* solution of potassium hydrate may be used; but the collector must be careful in employing this method, for the caustic nature of the alkali is apt to dissolve away the periostracum of the shell, in which the colouring matter alone exists.

In the case of a bivalve the animal is extracted by the use of the small blade of a pocket knife, or, better still, a small dissecting scalpel, taking care, in doing so, not to cut the ligament which holds the valves of the shell together. Then, having well cleaned the shell, twist it up tightly in paper, so that the ligament may dry and the valves become firmly set. If this is not done, the valves will gape.

Slugs should be killed by drowning, and their mucus removed by careful rubbing with a cloth. They may may then be transferred to glass tubes filled with some medium for their preservation. Several media for this purpose have been recom-mended. I use a weak solution of chloride of zinc; but turpentine, or a mixture of equal parts of glycerine and methylated spirit, may be used in the absence of this. Mr. Woodward employs a solution of calcium chloride, made by dissolving white marble in hydrochloric acid until all effervescence ceases, and a saturated solution is obtained.

But by far the most preferable method—and it is the one I always pursue now—was described by M. E. Dubreuil in an article entitled " Procédé pour la préparation des Limaciens," which appeared in " La Journal de Conchologie," for 1864, pp. 243-245. The animal is first killed and washed in pure water, to which, after the lapse of six or eight hours, some salt is added. A slit is then made along the *left* side, and the animal skinned. Thus, by means of two more longitudinal slits, three preparations can be made— one to show the back, one the foot, and the third the right side with the pulmonary orifice. These are glued on cardboard, varnished with white shellac varnish, to which a little corrosive sublimate has been added, and duly labelled.

In conclusion, do not go to the unnecessary expense of buying a special cabinet for your shells. Lay them on cotton wool, in cardboard trays, having one tray to each species or variety. These trays may then be stored away in boxes for future reference. And never forget to label your specimens, writing on each label the scientific name—and, when requisite, the varietal name in addition—of the species, locality, and date of capture.

CHAPTER IV.

CONSPECTUS OF THE CLASSES, ORDERS, FAMILIES, AND GENERA OF BRITISH LAND AND FRESH-WATER SHELLS.

CONSPECTUS OF THE CLASSES, ORDERS, FAMILIES AND GENERA OF BRITISH LAND AND FRESH-WATER SHELLS.

(AQUATIC)

CLASS I.—MALACOZOA ELATOBRANCHIA, MENKE.

Shell a bivalve, the two valves of which are united along their dorsal margin by a ligament. Body oval, headless; mantle bi-lobed; foot linguiform, sometimes provided with a byssus. Respiration accomplished by gills.

ORDER I.—LAMELLIBRANCHIATA.

Gills four, leaf-shaped, and arranged in pairs on each side of the body.

FAMILY I.—**Sphæriidæ.**

Shell equivalve, subglobose ; hinge with lateral and cardinal teeth. Body with one or two siphons at its *anterior* end.

1. **Sphærium,** Scop.—Shell nearly equilateral. Mantle with two prominent contractile siphons.

2. **Pisidium**, C. Pfr.—Shell inequilateral. Animal with one siphon.

FAMILY II.—**Unionidæ.**

Shell large, oblong, equivalve, inequilateral. Mantle·

lobes free all round, except at the posterior edge, where they form two subuliform orifices.

3. **Unio**, Philippsson.—Shell firm and solid, cardinal teeth large, lateral teeth lamelliform.

4. **Anodonta**, Lamarck.—Shell thin, hinge *edentulous*.

Family III.—Dreissenidæ.

Shell boat-shaped, somewhat triangular, equivalve, furnished with a byssus; umbones placed at the extreme end; hinge with small teeth or edentulous; ligament internal.

5. **Dreissena**, Van Ben.

CLASS II.—MALACOZOA GASTROPODA, CUV.

Shell univalve or none (internal). Body with a distinct head, and two or four tentacles; eyes situated at the extremity of the dorsal tentacles, or at the base of them; respiration effected by gills or lung.

ORDER I.—PECTINIBRANCHIATA.

Shell spiral, external, operculated. Respiratory organ consisting of a single pectiniform gill.

Family I.—Neritidæ.

Shell semiglobose; spire small, flat, excentric, mouth semicircular; operculum shelly, with a plate-like appendage on its under side.

1. **Neritina.**—Lam.

Family II.—Paludinidæ.

Shell cone-shaped, venticose; mouth oval; operculum concentrically striated. Body oval; eyes sessile or placed on pedicels at the base of the tentacles; gill internal.

2. **Paludina,** Lam.—Animal ovoviviparous; eyes placed on pedicels; operculum horny.

3. **Bythinia,** Gray.—Animal oviparous; operculum shelly.

4. **Hydrobia,** Hartm.—Operculum horny, thin, paucispiral; eyes placed on tubercles.

Family III.—Valvatidæ.

Shell conoid, more or less depressed; mouth circular; operculum horny, multi-spiral. Body spiral, with two tentacles, and provided with a long, plumelike gill, protruded when the animal is crawling; eyes situated on the inner-side of the base of the tentacles.

5. **Valvata,** Müll.

Order II.—Pulmonobranchiata.

Shell generally spiral and external, but sometimes (*Limacidæ*) rudimentary and internal, or wanting. Body spiral, generally non-operculated, but sometimes with an operculum; respiration effected by means of a lung.

Family I.—Limnæidæ.

Shell spiral or hood-shaped; mouth edentulous. Tentacles two; eyes sessile.

6. **Planorbis,** Guettard.—Shell orbicular, flat, and coiled nearly in the same plane; mouth semicircular; umbilicus distinct; non-operculated. Tentacles two in number, very long; eyes sessile; foot oval and short.

7. **Physa,** Lam.—Shell spiral, thin, polished; spire sinistral; non-operculated. Animal with two long tentacles, with the eyes at their base; mantle very large so as to cover part of the shell.

8. **Limnæa,** Brug.—Shell oval, thin, translucent; mouth oblong; columella with an oblique plait; non-operculated. Animal with two short triangular tentacles bearing the eyes at their base; foot oval.

9. **Ancylus,** Geoffrey.—Shell conical, oblong, limpet-shaped; apex pointed and bent to the right; spire dextral or sinistral. Animal with two cylindrical tentacles, with the eyes at their base; foot large.

(TERRESTRIAL.)

Family II.—**Limacidæ.**

Shell placed under the mantle, rudimentary or shield-like. Body united in its whole length with the foot beneath, there being no 'visceral hump'; tentacles four, cylindrical, the dorsal pair bearing the eyes; mantle shieldlike.

10. **Arion,** Ferussac.—Shell consisting of loose calcareous granules. Mantle shagreened, not striated concentrically; respiratory orifice placed on anterior half of the mantle; tail provided with a slime gland.

11. **Geomalcus,** Allman.—Shell solid, unguiform, concentrically striated. Body capable of great extension; mantle finely shagreened; tentacles short, eyeless; respiratory orifice placed more anteriorily than in Limax; tail provided with a large slime gland.

12. **Limax,** Linn.—Shell oval or unguiform.

Mantle concentrically striated or granulated ; respiratory orifice situated on posterior half of mantle ; tail carinated, and without a slime gland.

(Subgenus, **Amalia**, Moq.—Mantle granulated. Subgenus, **Eulimax**, Moq.—Mantle concentrically striate.)

Family III.—Testacellidæ.

Shell small, auriculate, external, placed on the hinder portion of the body, covering the mantle ; respiratory orifice on the right side below the mantle.

13. **Testacella**, Cuvier.

Family IV.—Helicidæ.

Shell spiral. Body distinct from the foot; tentacles four, retractile, cylindrical, the upper pair being the longest, and bearing the eyes at their apices.

14. **Succinea**, Drap.—Shell oval or oblong, thin, transparent ; spire small ; mouth large and obliquely oval ; non-operculated. Animal not capable of entirely entering its shell.

15. **Vitrina.**—Drap. Shell subglobular, thin, flattened ; mouth large and semilunar ; umbilicus wanting.

16. **Zonites**, Montf.—Shell orbicular, depressed, umbilicated ; mouth obliquely crescent-shaped.

17. **Helix**, Linn.—Shell globular, convex, or flattened ; mouth more or less circular or oval ; outer lip generally thick, and possessing an internal rib, sometimes reflected and provided with tubercles or teeth ; umbilicus usually distinct.

18. **Bulimus**, Ehrenb.—Shell oval or oblong-

ovate; spire obtuse, but much more prominent than in Helix; mouth oval; umbilicus very small. Tentacles shorter than in **Helix.**

19. **Pupa**, Lam.—Shell cylindrical or oblong, with many narrow whorls; mouth oval or lunate, generally toothed within; peristome incomplete, thickened, reflected; umbilicus very minute.

20. **Vertigo**, Müll.—Shell subcylindrical, with closely pressed, gradually enlarging whorls; mouth more or less angular, generally toothed internally; umbilicus minute. Resembles **Pupa**, but differs in having the ventral tentacles wanting, and in having the peristome thinner.

21. **Balia**, Prideaux.—Shell sinistral, elongated, thin; mouth ovate, sometimes with a denticle on the base of the penultimate whorl; peristome thin; umbilicus narrow.

22. **Clausilia**, Drap.—Shell sinistral, fusiform; mouth pyriform or elliptical and toothed, furnished with a clausilium*; umbilicus very small.

23. **Cochlicopa**, Ferrussac.—Shell oblong or oblong-oval, very glossy, transparent; mouth pyriform; outer lip thickened but not reflected.

24. **Achatina**, Lam.—Shell cylindrical, smooth,

---

* The clausilium is a shelly plate attached to the columella by an elastic ligament about half a whorl from the mouth, and may be best seen by breaking away the outer part of the body whorl. It serves the same function as an operculum, but it is not, as in that structure, fastened to the animal. When the animal extends itself out of the shell the clausilium is pushed against the columella, and when it withdraws, the clausilium flies backwards on account of the elasticity of its ligament, and closes the mouth of the shell.

thin, glossy; mouth oval, with a notch at its base; outer lip thin and not reflected; umbilicus wanting.

FAMILY V.—Carychiidæ.

Shell spiral, oblong; mouth oval, dentated; umbilicus very minute. Eyes situated at the hinder base of the dorsal tentacles; lower tentacles rudimentary.

25. **Carychiidium,** Müll.

FAMILY VI.--Cyclostomatidæ.

Shell cylindrical or conical, operculated; mouth round or oval; operculum testaceous or horny.

26. **Cyclostoma,** Drap.—Shell conical; operculum testaceous.

27. **Acme,** Hartm.—Shell cylindrical; operculum horny.

DESCRIPTIONS OF THE SPECIES AND VARIETIES OF BRITISH LAND AND FRESH-WATER SHELLS.

SPHÆRIUM CÓRNEUM. LINN.

SHELL suborbicular, or rounded-ovate, equilateral, with fine concentric striations, brownish, or yellowish-brown; umbones broad and blunt, and nearly central in position; ligament short, and not visible externally; muscular impressions scarcely visible: hinge strong, with a double cardinal tooth in each valve, and two lateral teeth of a triangular shape in the right valve, and four teeth in the left valve. Animal greyish, sometimes reddish or brownish: siphons pale grey, elongated, truncate. Length 6 lines; breadth 4 lines; thickness 3½ lines.

Habitat.—Ditches, marshes, ponds, canals, and rivers.

v. flavescens. (*Macgill.*); Paler, not so large, and more globular. (= *C. flavescens*. Macgillivary. *Moll. Aberdeen*, p. 246.)

v. nucleus (*Stud.*): Smaller and nearly spherical. (= *C. nucleus*. Studer, *Kurz. Verzeichn*, p. 93.)

v. Scaldiana (*Norm.*): Ovate, paler. (= *C. Scaldiana* Norm. *Cycl.*, p. 5, f. 1, 2.)

v. Pisidiodes (*Gray*): Shell subtriangular, slightly more produced at its posterior slope, ligament only

just visible externally, transverse striæ coarser. (= *S. Pisidiodes*, Gray. *Ann and Mag. Nat. Hist.* July, 1856.)

v. compressa (*Gray*): Shell rather compressed, margins meeting at an acute angle.

v. minor (*Gray*): Shell smaller, and nearly globular.

v. brunneo-fasciata (*Williams*): Shell paler than type, with the umbones shaded with brown colour, in which there are three just discernible bands forming segments of a circle, and of a darker brown. Externally to these, and separated by a band of ground-colour, is another similar band of the same tint as the others, but much better defined in outline.

SPHÆRIUM RIVICOLA, LEACH.

SHELL larger than S. corneum, S. ovale, or S. lacustre, oval-ventricose, brownish green, or yellowish horn-colour, with two or three darker bands and strong concentric ridges; umbones central, blunt; ligament very conspicuous on the outside: muscular scars distinct; teeth and hinge as in S. corneum, but stronger. Length of shell 10 lines; width 7 lines; thickness 5 lines.

Habitat.—Canals and sluggish streams.

SPHÆRIUM OVALE, FERUSSAC.

SHELL oblong, compressed, pale drab or yellowish in colour, with faint concentric striæ; anterior side roundish; posterior side truncate, and sloping towards lower margin; umbones small, slightly prominent, and nearly central; ligament long, narrow, and visible externally; hinge-line straight on posterior, but incurved on anterior side; teeth as in S. corneum, but differing in having the cardinal teeth very small and difficult to see. Animal milk-white. Length of shell ½ inch; width ⅜ths inch; thickness ¼ inch.

Habitat.—Ponds and rivers. Local.

SPHÆRIUM LACUSTRE, MULL.

SHELL subrhomboidal, rounded or elliptical, much compressed, thin, yellowish-white, or ashy in colour, regularly striate concentrically; umbones central, narrow, prominent, and capped with the nucleus of the shell; ligament short, slightly visible externally; muscular impressions indistinct; hinge strong; teeth as in the other species, but smaller and shorter in proportion. Body whitish, or slightly rose-coloured; siphons elongated, the branchial one being cylindrical and truncated at its orifice. Length of shell 4 lines, width 3 lines; thickness 1½ lines.

Habitat.—Ponds and canals.

v. **Brochoniana** (*Bourg.*): Shell much larger and flatter; umbones, smaller and not so well pronounced. (=*S. Brochonianum* Bourguignat, *Monogr, Sphær*, p. 20, pl. 3, f. 1, 2, 3).

v. **rotunda** (*Jeff.*): Shell rounder and flatter: epidermis yellowish-green. (B. C. vol. i., p. ii.)

v. **Ryckholtii** (*Norm.*): Shell small, triangular, and globular; umbones very pronounced. (=*C. Ryckholtii*, Norm. *Cycl.* p. vii., f. v., vi).

PISIDIUM AMNICUM, MULL.

SHELL triangular, ventricose, solid, deeply grooved concentrically, whitish-grey, or pale brown in colour; anterior side very rounded; posterior side much produced, and sloping towards lower margin: lower margin arched; ligament short, narrow, conspicuous: teeth as in Sphærium, but, in this species, and in all the other Pisidiums, the lateral teeth are strong and developed in a direct ratio to the size of the shell; umbones blunt, rather prominent. Animal whitish or greyish; siphon short, conical, or cylindrico-conical, obliquely truncated at its extremity. Length of shell 4 lines; width 3 lines; thickness 1⅓ lines.

Habitat.—Canals, ponds, lakes, and rivers.

v. striolata (*Moq.*): Shell smaller, wrinkles more pronounced.

v. læviuscula (*Moq.*): Shell larger; wrinkles demi-effaced.

v. flavescens (*Moq.*): Shell of an unicolorous pale yellow.

PISIDIUM FONTINALE, DRAPARNAUD.

SHELL sub-triangular, thin, swollen, greyish-white, finely striated concentrically; anterior side abruptly truncated; posterior side rounded, and gently sloping towards the inferior margin; umbones prominent and pointed; ligament short and scarcely visible; hinge short, very strong; teeth the same as in last species, but with the exception that the cardinal teeth are not arranged in the shape of an inverted V; muscular scars deepish. Animal whitish, or greyish; siphon sub-conical, short, and obliquely truncated at the extremity.

E

Habitat.—Canals, ponds, ditches, and slow-running streams.

v. **Henslowana** (*Shepp*) : The valves with a plate-like appendage near the umbones.　(= *Tellina Henslowana.* Sheppard, *Linn Trans*, xiv.)

v. **pulchella** (*Jenyns*) : Shell more glossy, strongly grooved; umbones less acute.　(= *P. pulchellum.* Jenyns, p. 18, *tab.* xxi., f. 1—5.)

v. **pallida** (*Gassies*) : Shell more tumid and paler, with a few darker rays diverging from the umbonal region to the inferior margin, irregularly striate.

v. **cinerea** (*Alder*) : Shell larger and flattter; striæ fainter.　(= *P. cinereum,* **Alder,** *Suppl. Cat. Moll. Northumb.*, p. iv.)

PISIDIUM PUSILLUM, GMELIN.

SHELL oval, thin, compressed but swollen, finely but irregularly striated, yellowish-white or greyish-horn colour; anterior side very rounded; posterior side very convex and sloping gradually downwards; lower border arched; umbones obtuse, short and nearly central; ligament short, narrow, and not visible from the exterior; hinge, teeth, and scars the same as P. fontinale.　Animal whitish or reddish ; siphon short, subconic or cylindrical, truncated.

Habitat.—Marshes, and ditches.

v. **obtusalis.** *(Lam)*: Shell smaller and much more tumid ; umbones sharp, pronounced.

v. **grandis** *(Adams)*: Shell much larger.

v. **ventrosa** (*Moq.*): Shell slightly more trigon-shaped, more ventricose.

v. **circularis** (*T. D. A. Cockerell*) : Shell greyish, rather shiny, almost circular in outline, subtruncate anteriorly ; umbones almost central; diam. 3 mill.

PISIDIUM NITIDUM, JENYNS.

SHELL suborbicular, in the upper part rather swollen, in all the other parts compressed, thin, very shining, finely and regularly striated; anterior side rounded and somewhat truncate; posterior side slightly produced and sloping abruptly downwards; lower margin rounded; umbones obtuse and subcentral with a few separate and deeper grooves surrounding them; ligament short, not visible from the exterior; hinge and teeth as in P. fontinale; muscular impressions distinct. Animal whitish; siphon short, funnel-shaped, with a plaited outer margin. Length of shell $\frac{1}{12}$ inch; width $\frac{1}{3}$th less.

Habitat.—Ponds and pools.

v. **splendens** (*Baudon! Mss. Moq.*): Shell lemon-coloured.

v. **globosa** (*Adams*): Shell sphæroidal.

PISIDIUM RÓSEUM, SCHOLTZ.

SHELL somewhat oblong or subrhombic, ventricose, thin, glossy, with deep and regular concentric striæ, yellowish-white or pale-horn colour; anterior side sloping abruptly downwards and truncate; posterior side produced and rounded; lower border almost straight; umbones very excentric, obtuse, prominent; ligament nearly invisible; cardinal and lateral teeth small; muscular impressions not well pronounced. Animal opaline white, orange-yellow or rose-colour in upper part; siphon subconic, long, truncated and without plaits.

Habitat.—Ponds and pools.

UNIO TUMIDUS, PHILIPPSSON.

SHELL ovato-oblong, wedge-shaped, swollen, moderately thick, solid, brown, often tinged with green in lines of growth; epidermis smooth; umbones prominent, rugose, excentric; lunule lanceolate, narrow; ligament short, thick, and prominent; anterior side rounded and sloping towards the front; posterior side produced and attenuated so as to become wedge-shaped; anterior teeth high, conical and strong. Animal greyish. Mantle bordered with brown; upper orifice elongated and of a brown colour; lower orifice pale grey. Length of shell 3 inches; width 1½ inches.

Habitat.—Canals, ponds, and slow-running rivers.

v. **radiata** (*Colb*): Shell thinner; epidermis greenish with yellow rays which are interrupted by bands of the same colour running transversely across the shell; posterior side more compressed above; hinge line nearly straight.

v. **ovalis** (*Mont.*): Shell wedge-shaped, dark olive-brown; anterior side broader, abruptly truncate; lunule broad, deep, oblique. (=*Mya ovalis*. Montagu, *Test. Brit.* pp. 34 and 563.)

UNIO PICTORUM, LINN.

SHELL ovato-oblong, wedge-shaped, ventricose, solid, greenish-yellow, marked with brown in lines of growth, and green-coloured towards the posterior margin; posterior side not wedge-shaped, but produced into a bluntly truncated beak; anterior side rounded; umbones not so prominent nor so rugose as in U. tumidus; lunule long,

narrow ; hinge line nearly straight ; anterior teeth arched, crenated, very much compressed; hinder teeth of left valve small or evanescent; ligament longer than in U. tumidus. Length of shell 2-3 inches.

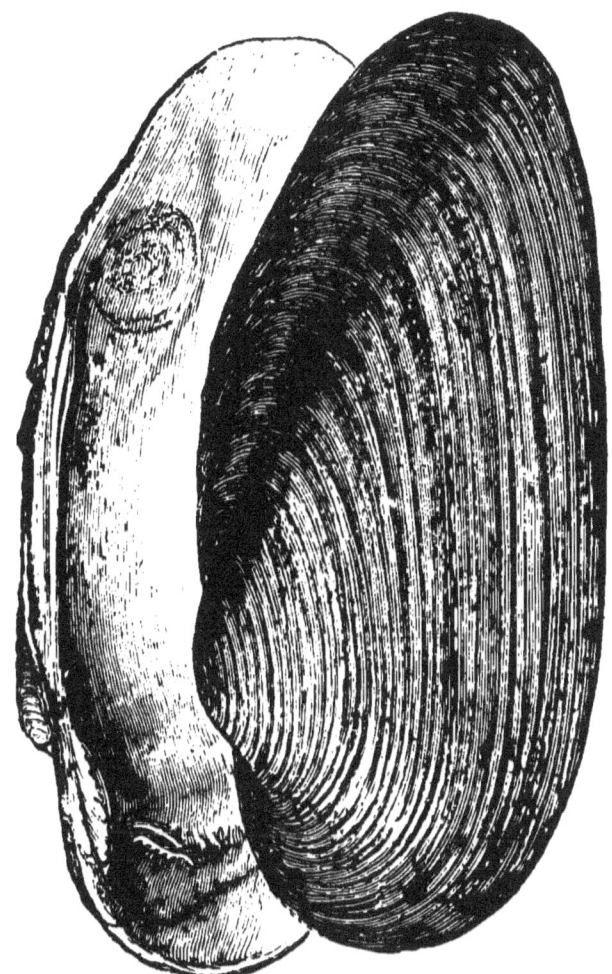

FIG. 1.—*Unio Pictorum.*

Habitat.—Ponds, lakes, and slow-running streams.
v. radiata (*Moq.*) : Shell yellowish, with green rays.

v. ponderosa (*Pasc.*): Shell very large, more elongated, narrowing towards its posterior extremity, more ventricose, thicker, brown.

v. curvirostris (*Norm.*): Shell smaller, shortened, bent, cuneate posteriorily, olive-coloured.

v. latior (*Jeff.*): Shell broader, shorter, yellowish-brown.

v. rostrata (*Lam.*): Shell slightly more elongated, lanceolate behind, brownish (= *U. rostrata*, Lam ! *Anim. Sans. Vert.* vi., 1, p. 77).

v. compressa (*Jeff.*): Shell broad and flat; upper margin raised and curved; posterior side greatly compressed and attenuated, assuming a beak-like form, and having a double ridge and furrow, which runs from the beak in the younger state of growth; lower margin straight; lunule broad, and extending between the beaks so as to separate them from each other.

UNIO MARGARITIFER, LINN.

SHELL elongate-ovate, thick, heavy, rather compressed, black brown, strongly striated in the line of growth; umbones excentric, incurved, and generally more or less extensively eroded; lunule indistinct and narrow; ligament very long, and extending to anterior side; anterior side rounded; posterior side gradually sloping, rounded at its extremity, and obtusely keeled above; lower margin straight; hinge strong; cardinal teeth small, slightly compressed, thick, subtriangular-conic, the posterior one of the left valve much developed. Animal dirty grey, more or less reddish. Length 5½ inches; width 2½ inches; thickness 1 inch.

Habitat.—Among the gravel and small stones in the shallows of quick-running rivers or mountain torrents.

v. **Roissyi** (*Mich.*): Shell less arched above, not sinuous below, larger posteriorily (= *U. Roissyi*, Mich., *Compl.*, p. 112, pl. xxvi., figs. 27 and 28).

v. **sinuata** (*Lam.*): Shell yellowish-brown, broader in proportion to length than type; lower margin incurved towards the middle (= *U. sinuata* **Lam.** *Hist. An. s. v.* vi., pl. 1, p. 70).

ANODONTA CYGNEA, LINN.

SHELL very large, oval, compressed in young but ventricose in old specimens, thin, glossy, dull green, more or
less tinged with a dusky tint; umbones small, convex;
lunule indistinct; umbonal region plaited; hinge-line
straight; ligament long; anterior side rounded, not
gaping, and abruptly sloping downwards: posterior side
compressed above, gaping, and produced into a rounded
cuneiform point; lower margin straightish. Animal grey,
yellowish-grey, or reddish-grey.

Habitat.—Lakes, ponds, canals, and muddy rivers.

v. **radiata** (*Mull*): Shell larger, with yellow rays
(=*Mytilus radiatus*, Mull, *Verm. hist.*, ii., p. 209).

v. **incrassata** (*Shepp.*): Shell more swollen and solid,
olive brown; upper margin slightly curved on its posterior
side (=*Mytilus incrassatus*, Shepp. *Linn Trans.* xii., p. 85,
pl. 5, f. 4).

v. **Zellensis** (*Gmel.*): Shell yellowish-brown, broader,
with the upper and lower borders nearly parallel; posterior
side much produced (=*Mytilus zellensis*, Gmel., *Syst. Nat.*,
1788, i., p. 3262).

v. **pallida** (*Jeff.*): Shell light yellow or fawn-colour;
hinge-line rather curved, and raised on the posterior side,
which is produced to a long wedge-like point; lower margin
rounded. (B. C., vol. i., p. 42.)

v. **rostrata** (*Rossm.*): Shell oblong-oval; upper margin
forming a dorsal crest, which is slightly raised and curved;
anterior side rounded; posterior side attenuated, and
ending in a long curved wedge-like point; lower margin
nearly straight. B. C., vol. i., p. 42. (=*A rostrata*
(Kokeil), Rossmässler, *Iconogr.*, iv., p. 25, f. 284).

ANODONTA ANATINA, LINN.

SHELL smaller than in A. cygnea, elliptical-oval in shape, compressed posteriorly, brown-olive coloured, irregularly-wrinkled, and with bands of a deeper hue in the lines of growth : umbones straight, excentric ; umbonal region compressed, rugose ; ligament short, prominent ; upper margin curved and raised into a sort of crest ; anterior side sloping obliquely towards the lower edge, rounded, and gaping ; posterior side curved, and sloping obliquely downwards to a wedge-shaped point ; lower margin gently curved ; muscular impressions more pronounced than in A. cygnea.

Habitat.—Small rivers, canals and ponds.

v. radiata (*Jeff.*) : Epidermis marked with green and yellow rays. (B. C. vol. i. p. 45).

v. ventricosa (*C. Pfr.*) : Shell very tumid in the middle and umbonal region, larger, more solid, marked with green and yellow rays. (=*A. ventricosa,* C. Pfeiffer, ii. p. 30, pl. iii.)

v. complanata (*Rossm.*) : Shell oval, very compressed, brown ; umbones close to anterior margin ; anterior side abruptly truncated ; upper margin raised and curved. (= *A complanata* (Ziegler) Rossmässler, p. 24, f. 283).

DREISSENA POLYMORPHA, PALLAS.

SHELL mussel-shaped, triangular, keeled in centre of both valves, flattened below, rather solid, olive or yellowish-brown, marked transversely on the upper part with zigzag streaks of purple or dark brown; umbones incurved, small, and placed at the anterior end; ligament long, narrow, and fitting into a sulcus in the hinge of each valve; hinge strong, toothless, with a hollow triangular plate under the umbones in both valves; upper margin angular; anterior margin nearly straight; posterior side curved; lower margin incurved. Animal blackish, furnished with a byssus.

Habitat.—Canals, lakes and rivers.

NERITINA FLUVIATILIS, LINN.

SHELL semi-globular, slightly oval, solid, glossy, yellowish or brownish, spotted with white, brown, purple or pink, and marked with fine but distinct plaits; spire short, lateral; composed of three whorls, the last one being excessively disproportionate; mouth transversely semilunar; operculum semilunar, yellowish, with an orange border, and underneath a strong, raised, grooved spire placed at one end. Animal white, head and back of the neck blackish; hinder part of the foot sometimes blackspotted; tentacle long, white, with blackish line.

Habitat—In canals and rivers with stony bottoms.

v. cerina (*Colb.*): Shell of an uniform straw-yellow colour.

v. nigrescens (*Colb.*): Shell black or blackish.

v. trifasciata (*Colb.*): Shell ornamented with three spiral dark bands.

v. undulata (*Colb.*): Shell with some transverse dark bands.

PALUDINA CONTECTA, MILLET.

SHELL globoso-conoid, very swollen; whorls seven, of an unicolorous brown-olive, marked with three brownish bands on the body whorl, and with two bands of the same colour on the two preceding whorls; spire blunt, mucronate; umbilicus narrow, distinct and deep; mouth of an obliquely rounded oval, slightly produced at the upper angle; suture very deep; operculum concave, thin, reddish-yellow, with fine concentric striæ, and the nucleus depressed so as to form a bulging on the under side. Young specimens are subglobose, obscurely banded, flattened a little above, and furnished with five ciliated lines. Animal dark grey, black, or brown, spotted with yellow.

Habitat.—Canals and stagnant waters.

v. virescens (*Jeff.*) : Shell greenish.

PALUDINA VIVIPARA, LINN.

SHELL conically oval; whorls six and a half, not so swollen as in P. contecta, and with the sutures not so deep in consequence; dull yellowish-green, with three broad brown spiral bands on the body whorl, and two upon each of the preceding whorls; umbilicus represented by a narrow slit behind the inner lip; mouth oval and not quite so circular as in P. contecta; peristome continuous; operculum rather thick, horny. Animal dark grey, or brown, speckled with yellow.

Habitat.—Ponds, lakes, canals and slow rivers.

v. unicolor (*Jeff.*) : Bandless.

v. atro-purpura (*Lloyd*) : Shell like the type, but of a black colour, which, when viewed by transmitted light, is dark purple.

v. albida (*N. and T.*) : Shell white.

BYTHINIA TENTACULATA, LINN.

SHELL ovoid, or of an elongated-ovoid, sometimes sub-
conoid, rather glossy, thin, solid, subtransparent, yellowish
horn-coloured; whorls six, the body whorl large; mouth
oval, angular behind; umbilicus none; operculum oval,
thick, angulated above, and closely fitting. Length of
shell ½ inch; width $\frac{3}{10}$ths inch. Animal blackish, spotted
with gold colour; foot two-lobed in front, narrow and
subacute behind; tentacles long, setaceous; eyes black,
large, and sessile.

Habitat.—Streams, ditches, and canals.

v. **ventricosa** (*Menke*): Shell more tumid, globular-
conical in shape, white (= var. *a ventricosa*, Menke).

v. **excavata** (*Jeff.*) : Whorls more rounded, and suture
much deeper. (B. C., vol. i., p. 61.)

v. **albida** (*Rimmer*): Shell white.

v. **producta** (*Menke*): Shell less tumid, in shape
an elongated cone. (Drap., fig. 19. *Var. b. producta*
Menke).

v. **rufescens** (*T. D. A. Cockerell*): Shell red-brown.

m. **decollatum** (*Jeff.*): Upper whorls wanting in half-
grown and adult specimens; their place being supplied
by a nearly flat and semi-spiral plate, as in *Bulimus
decollatus*. (B. C., vol. i., p. 61).

BYTHINIA LEACHII, SHEPPARD.

SHELL conoid, very swollen towards the base, yellowish
horn-coloured; whorls four to five, very tumid, rounded,
distinctly separated by a deep suture; mouth nearly
circular, much less angular behind than in B. tentaculata;

umbilicus small, oblique; operculum nearly circular, flattish, and with the nucleus central. Length of shell ¼ inch; width 2 lines. Animal whitish, with black and yellow spots visible through the shell.

Habitat.—Ditches, canals, and sluggish rivers.

v. elongata (*Jeff.*): Shell smaller; spire more produced. (B. C., vol. i., p. 62).

v. albida (*Rimmer*): Shell white.

HYDROBIA SIMILIS, DRAPARNAUD.

SHELL ovoid, swollen, sub-opaque, pale horn-coloured; whorls five to six, very convex; sutures very deep and grooved; umbilicus represented by a narrow and oblique chink; mouth oval; operculum horny, concentric, with the nucleus lateral. Animal dark grey, tinted with yellow or brown, and speckled with flaky white.

Habitat.—In ditches between Greenwich and Woolwich which are flooded by the tide.

HYDROBIA VENTROSA, MONTAGU.

SHELL forming a lengthened cone, yellowish horn-coloured, thin, glossy, semi-transparent; whorls six to seven, swollen; spire long; suture not channelled as in H. similis; mouth oval; umbilicus smaller than in H. similis. Size half that of H. similis. Animal dark grey with black and grey rings round the tentacles.

Habitant.—In estuaries and in brackish water, or upon the mud banks of tidal rivers.

v. **minor** (*Jeff.*) : Shell smaller, spire shorter.

v. **decollata** (*Jeff.*) : Shell slightly eroded; spire truncate.

v. **ovata** (*Jeff.*) : Shell having a much shorter spire, consisting of only four whorls, which are more swollen than usual, and the last considerably exceeds one-half of the shell.

v. **elongata** (*Jeff.*) : Shell having its spire propor-tionally longer, with sometimes as many as eight whorls.

v. **pellucida** (*Jeff.*) : Shell clear white, nearly trans-parent.

VALVATA PISCINALIS, MULLER.

SHELL globular, thin, light horn-coloured, very finely spiral-striate, and marked with some obscure concentric lines; whorls five to six, rounded, the body whorl being very large; spire obtuse, compressed: mouth circular, with a complete peristome; umbilicus deep; operculum greyish-white, circular. Length of shell ¼ inch; width ¼ inch. Animal yellowish-grey, with slightly apparent milk-white specks.

Habitat.—Bottom of shallow muddy streams, on marsh lands, or on aquatic plants in ditches and canals.

v. **depressa** (*C. Pfr.*) : Spire more depressed; umbilicus larger. (= *V. depressa*, C. Pfeiffer, *Deutsch Moll.* 1, p. 100, pl. ii., fig. 33.)

v. **subcylindrica** (*Jeff.*): Shell having the spire more produced and flattened at the top; umbilicus small. (B. C., vol. i., p. 72).

v. **acuminata** (*Jeff.*) : Shell having the spire still more produced, and ending in rather a sharp point. (B. C. vol i., p. 73).

v. **pusilla** (*Mull.*): Shell smaller with stronger striæ, and with four to four and a half whorls (= *Nerita pusilla* Mull., *Verm Hist.* ii., p. 171.)

v. **albina** (*Taylor*) : Shell white or whitish.

m. **sinistrorsum** (*Jeff.*) : Spire reversed.

VALVATA CRISTÁTA, MULLER.

SHELL flatly-coiled, pale horn-coloured, striate transversely; upper surface slightly concave; under surface umbilicate so as to expose the interior convolutions; whorls five, the last being very large; mouth circular, and with a continuous margin; operculum round, slightly transparent, of a reddish horn-colour. Diameter of shell ¹⁄₀th inch. Animal dark grey or brown, slate-coloured underneath, and with a few black specks on its upper part.

Habitat.—Lakes, ponds, canals, and ditches.

PLANORBIS LINÉATUS, WALKER.

SHELL quoit-shaped, depressed, glossy, semitransparent, yellowish horn-coloured; whorls four, with two to five curved transverse plates inside the last whorl which appear as whitish lines when seen from the exterior; periphery obtusely carinated; mouth obliquely cordate. The last whorl is larger than the rest of the shell, and conceals nearly two-thirds of the penultimate whorl.

Animal brown with a reddish or violet tinge, sparsely speckled with black.

Habitat.—Slow streams and ponds in the home and eastern counties of England.

v. albina (*Taylor*): Shell milk-white and transparent.

PLANORBIS NITIDUS, MULLER.

SHELL depressed, discoid or quoit-shaped, thin, glossy, semi-transparent, yellowish horn-coloured, more or less reddish; upper surface more convex than the lower surface; whorls four to five, the outer whorl being very large in proportion to the rest, covering one-half of the preceding whorl, and obtusely carinated in the middle; suture deepish; umbilicus small, shallow. Diameter of shell, 2½ lines. Animal reddish-brown marked with fine grey specks.

Habitat.—On fallen leaves of trees, also on aquatic plants, in ponds and ditches.

v. albida (*Nelson*): Shell white.

v. minor (*Jeff. MS.*): Shell small.

PLANORBIS NAUTILEUS, LINN.

SHELL depressed, thin, subpellucid, rather concave above, rather convex below, dull light brown or grey, not glossy; periphery bluntly and indistinctly carinated; whorls three, the outer whorl strongly marked with transverse

F

ridges, and larger than the rest of the shell; mouth, oval; umbilicus large. Diameter of shell $\frac{1}{10}$th inch. Animal grey, marked with minute black specks.

Habitat.—In still waters on aquatic plants.

v. crista (*Linn.*): Shell with the transverse ridges more pronounced, and with the periphery deeply notched or crested by them. (= *Nautilus crista.* Linn., *Syst. Nat.* ed. x., 1758., i., p. 709. *Planorbis cristatus.*, Drap., *Hist. Moll.*, 1805, p. 44, pl. ii., figs. 1-3.)

PLANORBIS ALBUS, MULLER.

SHELL thin, pellucid, whitish, convex above, concave below, finely striated longitudinally, and marked with very fine close-set raised circular striæ which are clothed with deciduous bristles; whorls five, the last one being disproportionally enlarged; mouth roundish-oval: umbilicus large. Diameter of shell $\frac{1}{4}$ inch. Animal greyish-white, or greyish-brown; tentacles pale grey, with a central brown line; foot narrow, dark reddish-brown.

Habitat.—Lakes, ponds, and stagnant water.

v. draparnaldi (*Shepp.*): Shell more closely striate in line of growth; periphery distinctly carinate; umbilicus deeper. (= *P. spirorbis.* Drap. *Hist. Moll.* p. 45, pl. ii., f. 8-10.—*Helix Draparnaudi*, Sheppard. *Linn. Trans.* xiv., p. 158.)

PLANORBIS GLABER, JEFFREYS.

SHELL somewhat convex above, with a central depression, concave below, smooth, semitransparent, brownish horn-coloured; whorls five, rounded, and having the upper side more convex than in P. albus, the body whorl occupying nearly one-half of the shell; mouth nearly circular; suture well pronounced; umbilicus large; circular striæ absent. Body yellowish-grey.

Habitat.—Ponds, marshes, and lakes.

v. **compressa** (*Lloyd*) : Shell more concave below than in the type, and only depressed in the centre on the upper side; the whorls also are rounder, and do not increase so quickly, making the whole shell more compact.

PLANORBIS SPIRORBIS, MULLER.

SHELL concave above, flat below, *or the reverse*, thick, horn-coloured; whorls five to six, rounder, and with the keel not so well pronounced as in P. albus, the body-whorl not exceeding ⅛th the length of the spire; mouth roundish; peristome often white-ribbed; umbilicus wide, but shallow. Animal grey, tinged with purple or red.

Habitat.—Shallow and stagnant water, sluggish streams.

v. **ecarinata** (*Jeff.*): Shell smaller, light grey, having one whorl less than usual, and no trace of a keel. B. C. vol. i., p. 87. (=*P. spirorbis*, Moq. Tand, *Moll. Fr.*, p. 437, pl. xxxi., f. 1-5.)

v. **albida** (*Nelson*): Shell white.

m. **scalariforme** : Shell reversed.

PLANORBIS VORTEX, LINN.

SHELL concave above, flat below, extremely depressed, thin, pellucid, glossy, brownish horn-colour, marked with fine and regularly disposed striæ in line of growth; whorls six to eight, gradually increasing in size; the outer whorl rounded so as to form a sharp keel on its lower margin; mouth rhombic, compressed; umbilicus large and shallow. Diameter of shell ⅜ of an inch. Animal violet-brown.

Habitat.—Shallow and stagnant waters.

v. **compressa** (*Mich*): Shell thinner, flatter; keel more distinct, sharper, and placed nearly in middle of periphery. (=*P. compressus*, Mich., *Compl.* p. 81., pl. xvi., figs. 6-8).

F 2

PLANORBIS CARINATUS, MULLER.

SHELL nearly flat above, rather convex below, gradually shelving to the outer edge, thin, glossy, yellowish horn-colour; whorls five to six, the outer one growing suddenly larger; suture deep; periphery prominently keeled in the middle line; mouth obliquely oval, somewhat angular; umbilicus small, central. Animal deep reddish-brown, indistinctly spotted with black.

Habitat.—Stagnant waters, and sluggish rivers.

v. disciformis (*Jeff.*): Shell flatter and thinner, of a yellowish colour, having the last whorl larger in proportion to the others, and the keel more prominent and sharp, and placed exactly in the middle. (Jeffreys, *Linn. Trans.* xvi., pp. 385 and 521).

v. albida (*Hudson*): Shell pellucid white.

PLANORBIS COMPLANATUS, LINN.

SHELL brown horn-coloured, striolate, slightly concave above, flattish, with a central concavity below; whorls five to six, rapidly enlarging, ventricose, the diameter of the body whorl being equal to one-fourth of the whole; periphery strongly keeled below; suture deep; mouth rhombic, rounded in front, often ribbed internally; umbilicus large and very shallow. Diameter of shell ¾ of an inch. Animal deep violet-red, finely speckled with black.

Habitat.—Ponds, canals, ditches, and slow rivers.

v. rhombea (*Turton.*): Shell smaller, more convex above, with· a deep concavity beneath, and a blunt keel. *Helix rhombea*, Turton., *Conch. Dict.* p. 47. (Possibly these are the young of P. complanatus, and not a variety at all).

v. albina (*Jeff.*): Shell whitish or colourless. (B. C. vol. i., p. 91).

m. terebrum (*Turton.*): Whorls dislocated from one

another, and elevated into a spiral cone, (= *Helix cochlea.* Brown. *Wern. Trans.* ii., t. 24, f. 10.—*Helix terebra.* Turton. *Conch. Dict.* p. 62, f. 55).

PLANORBIS CORNEUS, LINN.

SHELL reddish brown in colour, sometimes white, glossy, nearly opaque, obliquely striate; whorls five to six, rounded above and below; periphery not keeled; suture deep; mouth semilunar; umbilicus broad and shallow. Diameter of shell ½– 1 inch. Animal nearly black.

Habitat.—Muddy streams, marshes, ponds, and ditches.

1. v. albina (*Jeff.*): Shell perfectly white. (B. C., vol. i., p. 94.)

2. v. albinos (*Moq.*): Shell whitish, very transparent. (Moq. Tand. *Hist. Nat. Mollusques de France,* p. 445.)

PLANORBIS CONTORTUS, LINN.

SHELL nearly flat above, with a deep concavity in the middle, deeply umbilicate below, solid, opaque, yellowish or brown-horn colour; whorls eight, compact and narrow; suture deep; mouth crescent-shaped, very narrow; umbilicus large and deep. Diameter of shell $\frac{2}{10}$ths inch; thickness $\frac{1}{10}$th inch. Animal grey or blackish.

Habitat.—Lakes, ponds, and ditches.

v. albida (*Jeff.*): Shell nearly white. (*B. C.,* vol. i., p. 95.)

v. excavata (*T. D. A. Cockerell*): Shell much depressed, and sunken above.

PLANORBIS DILATATUS, GOULD.

" THE shell is about the same size as P. nautileus, which may be considered its nearest ally; but it has one whorl

less, the periphery is angulated, the under side is remarkably gibbous, the mouth is very large, squarish, and
scarcely oblique; the outer lip is expanded ('so as to make
it trumpet-shaped'—Gould), and the umbilicus is abruptly
contracted, small and deep.   Body dark grey, often with
a slight orange tint, closely and minutely speckled with
flake-white; mantle thick, lining the mouth of the shell;
head large and tumid; mouth furnished with broad
lobular lips; tentacles cylindrical and extensile, widely
diverging, broad and triangular at the base.   The sheath,
or outer part, is gelatinous, and the core, or inner part, is
of a much darker colour, and apparently greater con-
sistence; tips rounded; eyes sessile on the inner base of
the tentacles; foot oblong, squarish in front and bluntly
pointed behind; verge curved on the left hand, or umbilical side of the shell."—(Dr. Gwyn Jeffreys, *Ann.* and
Mag. Nat. Hist., November, 1869.)

Habitat.—In the canals round Manchester.   Introduced
from America in cotton bales.

PHYSA HYPNORUM, LINN.

Shell sinistral, fusiform, with an elongated spire ending obtusely, thin, very glossy, covered with an epidermis, yellowish or reddish horn-coloured; whorls six to seven, rounded, body-whorl larger than the rest of the shell; suture shallow; mouth oval-lanceolate; pillar slightly sinuate. Length of shell $\frac{1}{2}$–$\frac{3}{4}$ inch. Animal blackish; mantle simple, and not covering the shell.

Habitat.—Ponds, ditches, and slow-running streams.

v. **major** (*Charp.*): Shell larger, more coloured. Height 10–13 mm. (= v. *b.* Charp., *Moll. Suiss.*, p. 19, pl. ii., fig. 12.)

v. **angulata** (*T. D. A. Cockerell*): Shell with a bluntly angled periphery.

v. **cuprella** (*Rowe*): Shell spindle-shaped, highly polished, semitransparent, copper-coloured, faintly striate in line of growth; whorls six, convex, with last one far exceeding in size the rest put together; spire tapering, blunt at its extremity; suture not deep; mouth oval, contracted above; inner lip spread on columella, with a strong and thick fold on its lower side. Body very dark slate-coloured, with very minute spots of a lighter colour, truncate in front, tapering to a point behind; edges slightly lighter than body-colour; tentacles long, slender, tapering, widely divergent.

m. **decollatum** (*Nelson*): Spire decollated.

PHYSA FONTINALIS, LINN.

Shell sinistral, oval, not covered with an epidermis, semi-transparent, thin, glossy, pale, greyish horn-coloured; whorls four to five, tumid, the first three extremely small, the last one occupying $\frac{3}{4}$ths or $\frac{4}{5}$ths of the shell; suture deep; spire extremely short; mouth oblong and wider and larger in proportion than in P. hypnorum; columella sinuate. Length of shell $\frac{1}{2}$-inch; width $\frac{1}{4}$-inch. Animal blackish-grey; mantle bilobed, one lobe of which is split into six,

Fig. 2.   *Physa Fontinalis.*

the other into nine digitate processes which, when expanded, lap over the shell.

Habitat.—Running brooks, canals, ditches, and sluggish rivers.

v. **inflata** (*Moq.*); Shell larger, more ventricose.

v. **curta** (*Jeff.*): Spire extremely short.   (=*Bulla fluviatilis*, Turt.   *Conch. Dict.*, p. 27.)

v. **oblonga** (*Jeff.*): Spire considerably produced.

v. **albina** (*Jeff.*): Shell milk-white in colour.

m. **dextrorsum** (*Williams*): Spire dextral.

PHYSA ACUTA, DRAP.

Shell of an elongated-ovoid shape, ventricose, somewhat glossy, with very fine longitudinal striæ, light horny, or whitish in colour; whorls three to five, a little convex, the last forming three-fifths of the total height of the shell; sutures moderately deep; apex acuminate; aperture obliquely

Fig. 3.—*Physa Acuta.*

and narrowly oval, acute superiorily; peristome interrupted, with the rudiment of an interior thickening. Alt. 8-16 mm.; diam. 7-9 mm.   Animal deep brown, covered with blackish spots.

Habitat.—In one of the lily tanks in Kew Gardens. Imported.

LIMNÆA GLUTINÓSA, MÜLL.

SHELL semi-globular, thin, transparent, amber or yellowish horn-coloured; whorls three to four, inflated, the last forming nearly the whole of the shell; spire slightly produced; suture rather deep; mouth oval; columellar fold curved, and sharp. Length of shell ½ inch. Animal of a pale, dull yellow colour, sprinkled with bright brimstone or whitish spots; mantle partly covering the shell.

Habitat.—Ditches, ponds, and lakes.

v. **mucronata** (*Jeff.*): Shell not quite so globular; spire more produced.

m. **intortum** (*T. D. A. Cockerell*): Spire very short and sunken, but slightly raised at the apex; body whorl swollen above. (*Vide* fig. 4.)

FIG. 4.—*L. Glutinosa.* m. *intortum.*

LIMNÆA INVOLÚTA, THOMPSON.

SHELL ovate, subglobose, thin, fragile, transparent, glossy, pale amber-colour; whorls three to four, convex, body whorl occupying the greatest portion of the shell; spire sunk within the last whorl; suture distinct, shallow; mouth pyriform, large; inner lip broadly spread on the penultimate whorl; columellar fold sharp, narrow. Maximum length 5½ lines; maximum breadth 3½ lines. Animal dark yellowish-brown, marked with flake-white specks at the sides of the head, tentacles, and foot.

Habitat.—A small alpine lake on Cromaglaun Mountain, Killarney, Ireland.

LIMNÆA PÉREGRA MÜLL.

SHELL oval, last whorl ventricose, thin, spirally striate,

varying in colour from pale yellowish-grey to dark red-dish-brown, whorls five, convex, the body whorl very large; mouth large, oval, and more than half the length of the shell; outer lip expanded; inner lip folded on columella, forming behind it a concealed narrow groove. Length of shell ½ to 1 inch; breadth ⅔rds of the length. Animal olive mottled with black and spotted with milk-white, black, and yellow.

Habitat.—Stagnant waters, and slow running streams.

v. Burnetti (*Alder*): Body a little broader than that of the typical form, dark olive, spotted with opaque yellow; mantle nearly black, with a few paler spots. Shell rather globular and solid, of a dull aspect, yellowish-brown, closely and strongly striate in line of growth; epidermis rather thick: the last whorl nearly covering all the others; exceedingly short, nearly truncate, and almost intorted. B. C., vol. i., p. 105 (= *Limnæa Burnetti*, Alder. *Ann. Mag. Nat. Hist.* N.S. ii., p. 396.)

v. solemia (*Zgl.*): Shell ventricose, whorls rounded, spire short, fauve-coloured, sub-transparent.

v. ovaliformis (*T. D. A. Cockerell*): Shell oval, glossy, semi-transparent, with close and well-marked striæ, the last whorl being very convex; spire a little less than half the length of the last whorl, moderately long and pointed; suture rather shallow; aperture oval, with a diameter rather more than half its length.

v. candida (*Porro*): Shell white.

v. stagnaliformis (*Taylor*): Shell somewhat fusiform in shape, the last whorl large, making about ⅔ths of the total length. Length 35 mill.; breadth 18 mill. Length of aperture 25 mill.; width 13 mill.

v. nitida (*Ziegl.*): Shell larger, slightly transparent, fauve.

v. ovata (*Drap.*): Shell ampullaceous, glossy, rather thinner; whorls very convex, the body whorl being very large; spire acute, very short; suture deep; aperture obliquely produced, ⅔ths the whole length of the shell.

[subvar decollata (*Fitzgerald*): With the apex decollated.]

Fɪɢ. 5. *Limnæa Peregra.* var. *labiosa.*

v. labiosa (*Jeff.*): Shell smaller, having the outer lip remarkably expanded and reflected. L. 0.5., B. 0.35. (B. C., vol i., p. 105.) *Vide* fig. 5.

v. lacustris (*Leach*): Shell small, thin, glossy, concentrically grooved; spire very short; aperture large. Body of a darker colour. (= *Gulnaria lacustris.* Leach *Moll. Brit. Syn.*, p. 107.)

v. lutea (*Mont.*): Shell very solid indeed; spire short, consisting of from 3-4 whorls (= *Helix lutea*, Mont. *Test. Brit.*, p. 180, tab. 16, f. 6.)

v. acuminata (*Jeff.*): Shell resembling v. ovata, except in having a more produced spire, and a smaller mouth. (B. C., vol. i., p. 105.)

v. intermedia (*Fér.*): Shell rather compressed towards the front margin, and thinner than usual; spire more produced; mouth expanded (=*Limnæa intermedia*, Fér. in Lam. *An. sans. vert.* vi., pt. ii., p. 162.) B. C., vol. i., p. 105.

v. oblonga (*Jeff.*): Shell oblong and compressed in front. (B. C., vol. i., p. 105.)

v. picta (*Jeff.*): Shell rather smaller than v. labiosa and beautifully marked by alternate bands of brown and white, which are sometimes confluent. (B. C., vol. i., p. 105.)

v. maritima (*Jeff.*): Shell dwarfed, rather solid; spire produced; suture deep. B. C., vol. i., p. 105.)

v. lineata (*Bean.*): Shell oblong, ovate, subventicose, with about twelve long and short (often forked) raised transverse lines on the body-whorl giving it an angular appearance, crossed by numerous longtitudinal striæ; whorls four; spire short and acute; aperture ovate; outer lip thin; inner lip reflected, forming a small hollow behind it. Length of the largest specimens 6 lines; breadth 4 lines (= *Limnæa lineata*, Bean. *Loudon's Mag. Nat. Hist.* vol. vii, p. 493).

v. **succinæformis** (*Jeff.*): Shell shaped like a *Succinea*, and very thin; whorls 4; spire small and oblique. (B. C., vol. i., p. 106.)

M. **decollatum** (*Jeff.*): Shell more or less eroded; spire truncate. (B. C., vol. i., p. 106.)

M. **sinistrorsum** *Jeff.*): Spire sinistral, rather solid; spiral ridges well pronounced. (B. C., vol. i., p. 106.)

M. **scalariforme** (*Jeff.*): Shell oblong, with deep and regular transverse striæ; whorls more or less disjointed; suture very deep. (B. C., vol. i., p. 106.)

LIMNÆA AURICULÁRIA, LINN.

SHELL globosely ovate, glossy, semi-transparent, yellowish horn-coloured, with deep and irregular lines of growth; whorls four to five, the last one being very much swollen, and occupying at least ⅞ths of the shell; spire very short and acute; mouth vastly expanded, roundish-oval, oblique; outer lip expanded; inner lip reflected, and forming a small umbilical chink behind it; columellar fold strongly curved and sharp. Animal dull greenish-yellow, mottled with black, and spotted with milk-white, black, and yellow.

Habitat.—Lakes, ponds, canals, marshes, and sluggish rivers.

v. **magna** (*Colb.*): Shell larger; aperture narrower, outer margin nearly parallel to the columella, which is straight, the upper edge reaching the commencement of the spire, which is sharp. Length 32 mill.

v. reflexa (*Nelson*): Shell with outer lip much reflected.

v. ampla (*Hartm.*): Spire short; aperture oval, extending beyond the apex. (= *Gulnaria ampla.* Hartm. *Gasterop*, 1842, p 69., pl. v.)

v. minor (*Moq.*): Shell smaller; aperture more oval.

v. Monnardii (*Hartm.*): Width of shell exceeding its height; spire rudimentary; aperture rounded, extending beyond the apex. (= *Gulnaria Monnardii*, Hartm., *l.c.*, p. 71., pl. vi.)

v. acuta (*Jeff.*): Shell smaller than the typical form, more oblong, and having the last whorl and mouth proportionably narrower. Body of a greyish colour, and closely covered with black spots. (= *Limnæus acutus*, Jeff., *Linn. Trans.*, xvii., p. 373.)

v. albida (*Jeff.*): Shell smaller and thinner, white, with a shorter spire, and less distinct striæ. L., 0·675., B., 0·55. (B. C., vol. i., p. 109.)

LIMNÆA STAGNALIS, LINN.

SHELL ovate-oblong, subulate, semi-transparent, thin, brittle, greyish-white, horn or brown-coloured; whorls six to eight, convex, the last one occupying nearly three-fourths the length of the shell: spire elongated to an acute point; suture deep; mouth oval; inner lip reflected on columella; columellar fold prominent and very much curved. Length of shell 1½ to 2 inches; breadth 1 inch. Animal yellowish, speckled with brown and milk-white.

Habitat.—In stagnant and slow-running waters.

v. fragilis (*Linn.*): Shell much smaller, narrower, thinner, amber-coloured. (= *Helix fragilis*, Linn., *Syst. Nat. Edit.*, x., 1758.)

v. roseolabiata (*Sturm.*): Shell slightly narrower, brown-black; aperture bordered interiorily with rose-violet.

v. scalariforme (*T. D. A. Cockerell.*): Whorls disunited. (*Vide* fig. 6.)

Fig. 6.—*L. Stagnalis.* var. *scalariforme.*

v. expansa (*T. D. A. Cockerell.*): Spire short, body-whorl large and expanded, mouth of the shell wide; the length of the spire is about ⅜ths of the total length of the shell, which is somewhat less than an inch and a half. (*Vide* fig. 7.)

Fig. 7.—*L. Stagnalis.* var. *expansa.*

v. variegata (*Hazay.*): Whorls variegated with opaque white markings.

v. decollata (*Simpson.*): Spire decollated.

v. elegantula (*T. D. A. Cockerell.*): Shell dark in colour, nearly scalariform; suture deep. (*Vide* fig. 8.)

v. albida (*Jeff.*): Like v. fragilis, but white in colour.

FIG. 8.—*L. Stagnalis.* var. *elegantula.*

FIG. 9.—*Limnæa Stagnalis*, VARIETY APPROACHING *L. Palustris* IN SHAPE.

LIMNÆA PALUSTRIS, MÜLL.

SHELL conic-oval, pointed, thick, opaque, varying in colour from yellow to dark violet brown, strongly striated in line of growth; whorls six to seven, convex, the last whorl occupying two-thirds the length of the shell; spire produced, ending in an acute apex; suture rather deep, circled by a narrow white line; mouth ovate, outer lip marked with brown or violet, inner lip expanded, and partially covering the slight umbilicus. Maximum length ¾ inch. Animal yellow-brown or cinereous, mottled with fine black and yellow spots.

Habitat.—Ponds, marshes, and lakes.

v. corva (*Gmel.*): Shell larger, swollen, opaque, blackish, violet-coloured within. (= *Helix corvus.*, Gmel. *Syst. Nat.*, 1788, p. 3658.)

v. fasciata *(Nelson)* : Shell of the same size and shape as the type, with three spiral bands of a darker brown colour on the body-whorl.

v. minor *(Taylor)* : Shell smaller, length 8 mill ; diam. 4½ mill.

v. elongata *(Moq.)* : Shell a little larger, slightly narrow, opaque, brown ; spire very produced.

v. lacunosa *(Zgl.)* : Shell with flattenings, depressions and protuberances. (= *Limnæus lacunosus.* Ziegl.)

v. disjuncta *(Moq.)* : Shell small, slightly turretted, thin, transparent, fauve ; whorls more convex ; sutures deeper. (= *Limnæa disjuncta?* Put., *Moll. Vosg.*, p. 60.)

v. obesa *(Taylor)* : Shell remarkable for its obesity, the dimensions of the type specimen being alt. 23 mill., diam. 14½ mill. ; apert. alt. 12½ mill. ; diam. 8 mill.

v. albida *(Nelson)* : Shell white.

v. roseo-labiata *(Jeff.)* : Mouth of the shell furnished inside with a rose-coloured or white rib. (B. C., vol. i., p. 114.)

v. tincta *(Jeff.)* : Shell shorter and broader, light brown, with a purplish mouth (= *Limnæus tinctus*, Jeff. *Linn. Trans.* xvi., p. 378).

v. conica *(Jeff.)* : Shell conic, greyish-white ; suture deep ; umbilical cleft present. (B. C., vol i., p. 114.)

m. angulatum *(S. C. Cockerell)* : Shell turretted, with five tumid whorls, bluntly angled at the periphery ; aperture oblong, and nearly twice as long as the spire. Length of shell 16 mill. ; breadth 10 mill. Length of aperture 10 mill. ; breadth 6 mill.

m. carinatum *(Taylor)* : Shell with a very strong keel ; spire slender and pointed. Length 11 mill. ; breadth 7 mill ; apert. length 5 mill. ; breadth 5 mill.

m. decollatum *(Jeff.)* : Spire decollated.

m. turritum *(T. D. A. Cockerell)* : Shell about half an

inch in length; whorls five; spire turreted; suture deep; last whorl more than half the total length of the shell,

Fig. 10.—*L. Palustris.* m. *turritum.*

and flattened at the sides, instead of being rounded as in a typical specimen. The upper whorls somewhat eroded.

LIMNÆA TRUNCATULA, MÜLL.

Shell oblong-oval, turreted, glossy, pale brown or yellowish horn-coloured, striated strongly in line of growth; whorls five to six, rounded, deeply separated from one another, and somewhat truncate above, the body whorl occupying about ⅜ths the length of the shell; spire produced; apex acute; suture very deep; mouth ovate-oblong, and nearly half as long as the shell; umbilical chink distinct. Length of shell ½-inch. Animal greyish, finely spotted with black.

Habitat.—Marshes, ditches, waterfalls, pools, and muddy streams.

v. **major** (*Moq.*): Shell larger, ashy, more tumid. Alt., 10-15 mm.

v. **minor** (*Moq.*): Shell smaller, horn-coloured.

v. **ventricosa** (*Moq.*): Shell same size as type, more ventricose; spire short; peristome without swelling.

v. **microstoma** (*Drouët*): Shell small, spire elongated, whorls more convex, aperture smaller and narrower (H. Drouët in Baudon, *Moll. Oise,* 1862, p. 14.)

v. **elegans** (*Jeff.*): Shell much larger, more solid and slender, greyish-white, marked with coarse spiral ridges : spire much produced; suture oblique; outer lip thickened. (B. C., vol. i., p. 116.)

G

v. albida (*Jeff.*): Shell smaller, milk-white. (B.C., vol. i., p. 116.)

m. scalariforme (*Jeff.*): Shell smaller; whorls nearly disunited. (B. C., vol. i., p. 116.)

LIMNÆA GLABRA, MÜLL.

SHELL an elongated cone, tapering, thin, glossy, with a few faintly marked longitudinal striations, horny or brownish; whorls seven to eight; mouth elongate-ovate, not above one-third the length of the shell, and with a broad internal white rib; umbilical cleft very minute. Length of shell 1 inch. Animal dark slaty grey, spotted with black.

Habitat.—Ponds and ditches.

v. major (*Gassies*): Shell much larger. Length 28 mill.

v. elongata (*Jeff.*): Spire more produced, so as to alter the relative proportions of length and breadth. (B. C., vol. i., p. 118.)

m. decollatum (*Nelson*): Spire decollated.

ANCYLUS FLUVIATILIS, MÜLL.

SHELL dextral, conoid, with the point recurved, and ex-
central, thin, yellowish-grey or horn-colour, and strongly
marked with regularly arranged striæ, which radiate from
the apex to the peristome, but more finely striate in line
of growth; mouth ovate, nearly a quarter of an inch in
diameter. Height of shell ¼-⅛th inch. Animal slaty-
grey, spotted with black, sinistral.

Habitat.—In streams and rivulets attached to stones,
or the shells of Unios and Anodons.

v. capuloides (*Jan.*): Shell elevated, very convex
anteriorily and laterally, nearly convex behind; aperture
oboval, rounded. (= *Ancylus capuloides.* Jan. in Porro !
Mal. Com. 1838, p. 87, pl. i., fig. 7.)

v. costata (*Fér.*): Shell whitish or greyish, ornamented
with very strongly marked striæ. (Ferussac. 1822, Art.
Ancyl. in *Dict. hist. nat. de Bory Saint-Vincent,* t. i.,
p. 436, No. 5.)

v. stricta (*Morelet*): Shell very elevated, very convex
in front, compressed laterally ; aperture elliptical, narrow.
(=*Ancylus strictus,* Morelet, *Moll. Portug.,* 1845, p. 88,
pl. viii., fig. 4.)

v. gibbosa (*Bourg.*): Shell slightly elevated, extremely
convex, sub-gibbous in front, convex laterally, nearly
straight posteriorly; apex obtuse, overhanging posterior
margin; aperture oboval. (=*Ancylus deperiditus,* Dup.,
Hist. Moll., 1851, v. p. 494, pl., xxvi., fig. 4 ; non Desm.—
A gibbosus, Bourg., *Cat. Ancyl,* in *Journ. de Conch.,* 1853,
p. 185.)

v. albida (*Jeff.*): Shell milk-white, and more finely
striated, (B. C., vol. i., p. 120.)

ANCYLUS LACUSTRIS, LINN.

SHELL sinistral, semi-ovate, with the vertex subcentral,
horn-colour, tinged with yellow or green, thin, glossy, com-

pressed at the sides; mouth ovate, sub-oblong, membranous.   Length of shell ¼ in.; breadth ¹⁄₁₆ inch.   Animal greenish-yellow, spotted with black; eyes sessile, round, black; tentacles cylindrical, obtuse and white.

Habitat.—Lakes, ponds, and sluggish streams, attached to water-plants, and the dead leaves of trees which have lain some time in the water.

v. **Moquiniana** (*Bourg.*): Shell elevated, very convex anteriorily, convex laterally and posteriorily; apex more crooked, slightly obtuse; aperture elliptical, narrow. (=*Ancylus Moquinianus*, Bourg., in *Journ. de Conch.*, 1653, p. 197, pl. vi., fig. 9.)

v. **compressa** (*Jeff.*) : Shell rather larger, and considerably broader and flatter than usual (B. C., vol. i., p. 122).

v. **albida** (*Jeff.*) ; Shell milk-white, with a light-grey epidermis (B. C., vol. i., p. 122).

ARION ATER, LINN.

SHELL composed of loosely aggregated calcareous granules. Body varying in colour from black to brown, yellow, and yellowish-white, rounded in front, attenuated behind, and covered with coarse and prominent tubercles; mantle finely shagreened; tentacles black, with the bulbs much swollen; foot marked with transverse black lines; slime yellowish. Length 2-5 inches.

Habitat.—Woods, thickets, gardens, and hedge-banks.

v. **Draparnaudi** (*Moq.*): Animal dark-red, foot-fringe yellowish or reddish.

v. **succinea** (*Mull.*): Animal yellowish, unicolor.

v. **bicolor** (*V. Brock*) *Moq.*: Animal dark brown, or blackish, sides yellowish or orange.

v. **nigrescens** (*Moq.*): Animal blackish, foot-fringe yellowish or reddish.

v. **marginata** (*Moq.*): Animal black, foot-fringe yellow, orange, or lead-coloured.

v. **pallescens** (*Moq.*): Animal dirty-white, a little reddish or yellowish.

v. **rufa** (*Linn.*): Animal red or brownish, unicolor. (=*L. rufus*, Linn, *Syst. Nat., Edit.* x., 1758, p. 652).

v. **albolateralis** (*Ashford*): Animal! dark-brown or blackish, with the sides white, and the foot-fringe orange; the two last colours being sharply defined from one another

v. **pallescens** (*Roebuck*): Animal light yellow.

v. **reticulata** (*Roebuck*): The rugosities are very pale, dirty-yellow, or nearly white, and the interstices between them grey, giving the whole body a beautiful and distinct reticulated appearance. The mantle is uniform grey, and the foot-fringe is pale and rather orange-tawny, with the usual black lines.

ARION FLAVUS, MULL.

SHELL white, opaque, wrinkled. Animal pale yellowish-grey; head, neck, and tentacles dark grey or blackish; mantle clearly granulated, more oblong than in A. ater, and marked with small white specks; respiratory aperture near the centre of the right margin of the mantle; tail angulated; slime yellow.

Habitat.—Among dead leaves, and decaying vegetable matter.

ARION HORTENSIS, FÉRUSSAC.

SHELL composed of granules cemented together into an oval mass. Animal smaller and more slender than A. ater, marked with longitudinal grey bands; mantle with a band round its margins, and one down its middle; edge of foot yellow, orange, or red-coloured; slime yellowish. Length, 1-1½ inches.

Habitat.—Woods, hedges and gardens.

v. fasciata (*Moq.*): Animal grey, with black bands.

v. rufescens (*Moq.*); Animal reddish, black bands.

v. grisea (*Moq.*): Animal pale grey, unicolor.

ARION SUBFUSCUS, DRAPARNAUD.

SHELL represented by a few isolated calcareous granules. Animal of a medium size and cylindrical in outline; reddish brown, with two lateral faint blackish bands; mantle very convex, slightly gibbous in front, paler than back, with two lateral black bands; tentacles blackish; back in its hinder portion subcarinated, and finely scaled; respiratory aperture nearly median; foot grey, marked with small transverse black lineoles; slime saffron-yellow. Length 40-60 mill.; width 60-10.

Habitat.—Woods and damp places.

v. **aurantiaca** : Animal bright orange, with ill-marked lateral bands.

ARION BOURGUIGNATI, MABILLE.

ANIMAL whitish-grey; back blackish, with lateral bands; keel well pronounced in young individuals, but becoming more and more obsolete as the slug becomes adult, and represented then by a pale line; foot whitish; length, 40 mill. (Mabille, *Rev. Zool.*, 1868).

Habitat.—Woods, gardens, and fields.

GEOMALCUS MACULOSUS, ALLMAN.

SHELL solid, flat, unguiform, marked with concentric lines of growth. Animal black, spotted with yellow, and covered with closely-set coarse tubercles; foot brown, transversely furrowed; sole light yellow, divided into three bands by a median longitudinal band of a paler colour; slime gland large.

Habitat.—West Kerry, Ireland.

AMALIA (LIMAX) GAGATES, DRAPARNAUD.

SHELL oval, rugous, thick from nucleus to centre; nucleus subterminal, blunt. Animal varying in colour from lead-grey and black to dark red, somewhat fusiform in shape; mantle granulated, oblong, bilobed, rounded behind, truncated somewhat anteriorily; dorsal tentacles dusty slate-colour, the ventral pair being paler; back distinctly carinated; slime colourless, thick, glutinous.

Habitat.—Gardens and hedgerows. Local.

v. **olivacea** (*Moq.*): Animal deep grey; olive-coloured.

v. **plumbens** (*Moq.*): Animal blackish-grey, more or less lead-coloured.

v. **rava** (*Williams*): Animal drab-coloured, slightly fuscous, with the mantle of a lighter colour than the back.

AMALIA (LIMAX) MARGINATA, MULL.

SHELL elliptical, slightly concave, lines of growth well pronounced; nucleus nearly terminal. Animal truncated in front, attenuated behind, reddish-brown or yellowish in colour; mantle of an elongated oval shape, granulated; head and tentacles dusky; keel prominent, always of a lighter colour than the rest of the back; slime colourless, glutinous.

Habitat.—Gardens and fields.

v. **rufula** (*Moq.*): Animal yellowish-red.

v. **rustica** (*Millet*): Animal greyish, mantle reddish, with a longitudinal black band on each side; mantle whitish.

EULIMAX (LIMAX) FLAVUS, LINN.

SHELL oblong or quadrangular, thin, concave; margin membranaceous; nucleus slightly prominent. Animal fleshy, yellow, tessellated with blackish-brown and white, coarsely tuberculated, keeled towards the end of its tail; mantle short, broadly rounded behind, concentrically striated; head, neck, and tentacles slate-colour; sole milk-white; foot-margin pale yellow; slime yellow.

Habitat.—Cellars and damp places.

v. **grisea** (*Roebuck*): Animal like the type, but with the ground-colour grey instead of yellow.

v. **suffusa** (*Roebuck*): Animal grey, unicolor.

v. **virescens.** (*Fér.*): Animal greenish, spots indistinct.

v. **colubrina** (*Pini.*): "Flavus, clypeo dorsoque late ac irregulariter nigro-maculato interstitiis flavis maculas nigras æquantibus."

EULIMAX (LIMAX) AGRESTIS, LINN.

SHELL small, oval, concave beneath, thin, rugose; nucleus small, slightly excentric; margin membranaceous. Animal generally yellowish, mottled with dusky and whitish, but varying greatly in colour; mantle large, broadly rounded behind, concentrically striated; back with a short keel, which is always placed obliquely; foot pale grey, or cream colour; slime milk white. Length $\frac{1}{4}$ to $\frac{1}{3}$ inches.

Habitat.—Fields, gardens, and woods. Widely distributed.

v. **nigra** (*Butterell*): Animal jet black, tentacles bluish or brownish-black, with the sole pale.

v. **filans** (*Hoy*): Animal greyish-white or ashy; mantle yellowish.

v. **punctata** (*Moq.*): Animal greyish or white, with very small black spots.

v. lilacina (*Moq.*): Animal lilac or brown-lilac, spotless.

v. albida (*Picard*): Animal greyish-white, spotless, with sometimes two lateral greyish-bands (scarcely obvious) on the mantle.

v. sylvatica (*Drap.*): Animal greyish, mottled.

v. cineracea (*Moq.*): Animal greyish-white, mantle ashy (=type).

v. reticulata (*Mull*): Animal red or reddish-grey, with irregular blackish spots.

v. nigricans (*Westerl*): Animal grey, variegated with black spots crowded together; tentacles and neck with a black line on the sides.

v. submaculata (*Williams*): Body greyish - white, streaked with seal-brown on the back, which extends on to the mantle and covers its posterior two-thirds; the sides of the body and the anterior third of the mantle are free from streaks and spotted with black.

v. tristis (*Moq.*): Animal brownish, mantle with two lateral brown bands, and sometimes a third intermediate band.

EULIMAX (LIMAX) LÆVIS, MULL.

SHELL unguiform, convex above, flat beneath, glossy, solid; margin sharp, slightly incurved, not membranous; nucleus terminal. Animal very glossy, dark brown tinged with violet, slender; mantle very tumid behind, pale yellowish-brown, nearly transparent; sole ash-coloured; respiratory orifice near the centre of the right margin of the mantle; slime almost colourless. Length $\frac{1}{2}$-$\frac{3}{4}$ inch.

Habitat.—In damp situations, under stones, and logs of wood.

v. maculata (*T. D. A. Cockerell*): Animal differing from the typical form in being spotted with dark brown.

EULIMAX (LIMAX) TENELLUS, MULL.

SHELL oval or oblong, somewhat tuberculous; margin broad, thin, membranaceous; boss indistinct, nearly terminal. Body rounded, compressed towards the tail, greenish white; head and tentacles black; mantle yellowish, rounded behind, concentrically wrinked; slime thick, orange coloured.

Habitat.—Woods in North Britain. Extremely local.

EULIMAX (LIMAX) ARBORUM, BOUCHARD-CHANTEREAUX.

SHELL oval, thin, nearly flat; margin membranaceous; nucleus small, subterminal. Body cinereous with yellowish-white spots, and a dusky band on either side, carinated near the tail; mantle concentrically striate, pointed behind; dorsal tentacles short; foot-margin white; slime colourless. Length $1\frac{1}{2}$–3 inches.

Habitat.—In woods on trees, especially the beech and walnut.

v. **Bettonii** (*Sordelli*): Animal ornamented on the back with white and fuscous spots; median band white, with two accompanying fuscous bands; median band on mantle white, with two alternating white and fuscous lateral bands; keel short.

v. **dicipiens** (*T. D. A. Cockerell*): Animal brownish-grey, with the markings coalesced so as to produce the appearance of pale spots on a dark grey ground; lateral bands ill-marked on mantle, none on body; keel short, dorsal line partly obsolete.

v. **maculata** (*Roebuck*): Animal with the ground colour as in type, but with the markings reduced to small and sharply defined black spots of a rounded or elongated form, and with a thin continuous band on each side which shows a tendency to break up into spots.

EULIMAX (LIMAX) MAXIMUS, LINN.

SHELL oblong, solid, flat, slightly concave; margin membranaceous; nucleus small, subterminal. Body large, varying in colour from ashy-grey to black, slightly carinated towards the tail; tentacles long, vinous coloured; mantle buckler-shaped, swollen, produced behind; slime whitish. Length 3–6 inches.

Habitat. — Cellars, gardens, woods, hedgerows, &c. Widely distributed.

v. cinerea (*Moq.*): Animal ashy, spotless, mantle bluish-black.

v. Ferrussaci (*Moq.*): Animal whitish, with four rows of black spots on mantle and body.

v. cellaria (*D'Argenville*): Animal ashy, mantle spotted with black, back with bands of the same colour, interrupted, and presenting alternating lines and points.

v. maculata (*Picard, Moq.*): Animal ashy, mantle and back with irregular black spots.

v. Johnstoni (*Moq.*): Animal ashy, mantle spotted with black; back marked with spots and two bands of the same colour. [Subvar lilacina (*Roebuck*): Animal resembling the type, except that the ground colour is lilac, instead of ashy.]

v. fasciata (*Moq.*): Animal of a deep ash colour with whitish bands, often five in number.

v. obscura (*Moq.*): Animal brown, unicolor.

v. rufescens (*Moq.*): Animal reddish, unicolor.

v. marmorata (*T. D. A. Cockerell*): Animal light greyish-brown; mantle marbled and spotted, darker in the anterior, and lighter in the posterior part (where it shades into a grey); the bands are grey, ill-defined, but fairly distinct, and there are black spots scattered here and there.

EULIMAX (LIMAX) CINEREO-NIGER, WOLF.

RESEMBLES closely Eulimax maximus, with which it was

till lately associated as a variety. It may, however, be distinguished by the following characters: The mantle is unicolorous and without markings; the pulmonary aperture is margined with the same colour as the ground colour of the body, but of a deeper tint; the keel is generally of a different colour from the rest of the body; and the sole is divided into three longitudinal bands, the middle one being white, and the two lateral ones dark.

Habitat.—Gardens and fields.

v. nigra (*Moq.*): Animal black, unicolor.

TESTACELLA HALIOTIDEA, DRAPARNAUD.

SHELL roundish-oval, ear-shaped, depressed; spire short, composed of one whorl and a half; suture deepish; mouth roundish, dilated in front.   Length of shell ¼-⅜ths inch. Animal dirty yellowish-brown, spotted with red, brown, white or black, capable of great extension; mantle small, covered by the shell; back rounded with two longitudinal furrows, which commence from the shell and terminate near the head; lips capable of being extended so as to simulate a third pair of tentacles.

Habitat.—Market gardens and fields.

FIG. 11.—*Testacella Haliotidea.*

v. scutulum (*Sowerby*): Animal yellowish; shell narrower in front than behind.   [Subvar, pallida (*T. D. A. Cockerell*): Animal pale yellowish, without markings. Subvar, aurea (*T. D. A. Cockerell*): Animal orange, with brown markings.]

TESTACELLA MAUGEI, FERUSSAC.

SHELL larger and more cylindrical than in T. haliotidea. Body dark brown-coloured.

Habitat.—Gardens and fields.

SUCCINEA PUTRIS, LINN.

SHELL ovate-oblong, smooth, glossy, transparent, very thin, irregularly striate, amber-coloured; whorls three to four, convex, body-whorl occupying four-fifths of the shell; mouth ovate, subvertical, two-thirds the length of the shell. Length of shell ½-¾ inch. Animal reddish-yellow.

Habitat.—Marshes, banks of ditches and pools, among flags, grasses, and sedges.

Fig. 12.—*Succinea Putris.*

v. vitrea (*Moq.*): Shell suboval, very thin, slightly yellowish, transparent. (=*Succinea virescens*, Morel).

v. Ferussina (*Moq.*): Shell small, slightly elongated, deep reddish-fawn coloured.

v. Charpentieri (*Dumont and Mortillet.*): Shell oval, slightly elongated, convex, thin, fragile, transparent, slightly glossy, light amber-coloured; spire short; whorls three, oblique, convex, separated from one another by a narrow suture, the last whorl, which makes up nearly the whole of the shell, is slightly narrowed in front; striæ large, irregular; aperture oval, narrow and acute above, much rounded in front; height 15 mill.

v. olivula (*Baud*): Animal pale yellowish-grey, shell having much analogy in shape to S. Pfeifferi, slender, oblong, narrow, very regularly conic, acute at the apex; spire very short; last whorl large, slightly contracted, and forming nearly the whole of the shell; aperture longly

rounded at the base, more narrow above; columella slightly concave in the middle, oblique, thin, transparent, fragile, crystalline, finely striated, pale or deep yellow amber-coloured with a greenish tint. Height 14-20 mill.

v. subglobosa (*Jeff.*): Shell shorter and broader in proportion to its length, usually much smaller and more solid. (B. C. vol. i., p. 152.)

v. vitrea (*Jeff.*): =*Succinea virescens*, Morelet. (*Vide infra*).

v. solidula (*Jeff.*): Shell much thicker, reddish-yellow. (B. C. vol. i., p. 152.)

SUCCINEA VIRESCENS, MORELET.

SHELL ovate-oblong, very thin, pellucid, greenish-yellow, concentrically striated; columella whitish; aperture ovate; spire very short. Length 10 mill., diameter 5 mill. Aperture 8 mill. long; 4½ mill. wide.

Habitat.—Marshes and ditch-banks.

SUCCINEA ELEGANS, RISSO.

SHELL smaller, more slender, and with a spire longer and more pointed than in S. putris, semi-transparent, amber-coloured. Animal yellowish-brown or black, making the shell, when containing the animal, appear of a greyish-blue, bluish, or greenish-black colour.

Habitat.—Generally found in company with S. putris.

v. minor (*Jeff.*): Shell reddish-brown, thinner; spire shorter; aperture more expanded.

v. ochracea (*Betta*): Shell smaller and thicker; spire longer; aperture smaller.

v. albida (*Taylor*): Shell white.

m. sinistrorsum (*Baud*): Whorls disjointed.

H

SUCCINEA PFEIFFERI, ROSSMÄSSLER.

SHELL oval, elongated, slightly curved at the extremities, transparent, pale yellow or reddish in colour; whorls three, twisted, the body-whorl occupying nearly the whole of the shell; spire short, conical, with the apex tuberculous; suture oblique, well defined, but not deep; aperture an elongated oval, acute above, rounded below, generally prolonged as far as ⅔rds of the total height of the shell. Length 12, diam. 6-7 mill. Aperture, 9 mill. long, 5 mill. wide.

Habitat.—Marshes and marshy places.

v. propinqua (*Baud*): Shell elongated, ventricose; spire short; body-whorl very large; aperture large, oval, elongated, occupying ⅔rds of the total height of the shell.

v. brevispirata (*Baud*): Shell short, moderately convex; spire extremely short; body-whorl occupying nearly the whole of the shell; aperture oval, rounded, elevated, moderately large, comprising at least ⅔rds of the total height of the shell.

v. ventricosa (*Baud*): Spire more elevated; body-whorl convex, large; aperture large, less elevated, being a little more than half the total height of the shell.

v. virescens *(T. D. A. Cockerell)*: Shell greenish; spire elongated; suture deep.

v. rufescens (*T. D. A. Cockerell*): Shell reddish; suture shallow.

v. intermedia (*Bean*): Shell yellow, acuminated oval in shape; spire prominent, rose-coloured; suture well-defined, deep; long. 9, diam. 5 mill; apert. 6 mill. long, 3 mill. wide.

v. elata (*Baud*): Shell very slender; spire long, very tortuous; body-whorl slightly convex, very contracted at its origin; aperture oval, slightly elevated, hardly one-half of the total height of the shell.

SUCCINEA OBLONGA, DRAP.

SHELL small, oval, ventricose, thin, fragile, light horn-coloured; whorls four, convex; suture deepish; spire produced, apex blunt; mouth oval and about the same length as the spire; somewhat resembles in shape Limnæa truncatula, but is distinguished from this species by the absence of the reflected lip on the columella.

Habitat.—Edges of ditches, near the coast, and on sand-dunes near the sea.

v. **humilis** (*Droüet*): Shell smaller, less elongated; aperture more rounded. (= *Succinea humilis*, Droüet.)

v. **arenaria** (*Bouch*): Shell oval, slightly oblong, ventricose, striæ very fine, thin, solid, slightly transparent, deep amber or reddish-horn coloured; spire composed of from one and a half to four whorls, very swollen and slightly twisted, the last whorl large; suture very deep; apex slightly pointed; aperture rounded-oval, exceeding in length one half of the total height of the shell. Height 6–8 mill.; diam. 5–6 mill. (= *Succinea arenaria*. Bouch. *Moll., Pas-de-Calais*, 1838, p. 54.)

VITRINA PELLUCIDA, MÜLL.

SHELL glassy-green, depressed, thin, glossy; whorls three to four, body-whorl very large; spire very short: mouth somewhat oval; umbilicus wanting. Height of shell ͺ½th inch; breadth ¼ inch. Animal elongated, too large to be contained entirely within the shell, pinkish-grey in colour; mantle finely spotted with black.

Habitat.—Among moss and dead leaves in woods and hedge-banks.

v. **depressiuscula** (*Jeff.*) : Shell rather oval, and flatter on both sides; spire scarcely raised above the level of the last whorl. (= *V. depressa* and *V. Draparnaldi*, Jeff. in *Linn. Trans.* xvi., pp. 326, 327.)

v. **Dillwynii** (*Jeff.*) : Shell nearly globular, with the last whorl very convex; spire more prominent. (= *V. Dillwynii*, Jeffr. *l. c.*, p. 506).

ZONITES CELLÁRIUS, MÜLL.

SHELL depressed, dirty-yellow or pale-horn colour, transparent, shining; under-surface clouded with white, especially about the umbilicus; whorls five to six; mouth crescent-shaped; umbilicus large, exposing the second whorl. Diameter of shell ¼ to ¾ inch. Animal dusky-grey.

Habitat.—Under stones in fields and woods, about walls in gardens, and in cellars. Universally distributed.

v. complanata (*Jeff.*): Shell smaller, spire flatter. (B. C. vol. i., p. 159.)

v. compacta (*Jeff.*): Shell more compact and convex; body-whorl less swollen, not so white beneath. (B. C. vol. i., p. 160.)

v. albinos (*Moq.*): Shell whitish.

ZONITES ALLIARIUS, MÜLL.

SHELL depressed, flat, pale amber or horn-colour, thin, transparent, very shining, upper surface smooth, and darker than the lower surface, which is not so white beneath as in the other species; whorls five, the last not so large in proportion to the others as in Z. cellarius; umbilicus moderately large, exposing the second whorl; aperture semilunar, narrow. Diameter ⅕th to ¼ inch. Animal darker than, but resembling Z. cellarius, emitting an alliaceous smell.

Habitat.—Walls, gardens and woods.

v. viridula (*Jeff.*): Shell greenish-white. (B. C. vol. i., p. 161.)

ZONITES GLABER, STUDER.

SHELL thin, very glossy, semi-transparent, compressed, convex above, less convex below, transversely striated,

darkish horn-coloured, with opaque white cloudings around
the umbilicus; whorls five to five and a half, convex, the
body-whorl occupying about one half of the shell; spire
slightly produced, with a blunt apex; suture not deep;
aperture forming three-fourths of a circle; umbilicus
narrow, deep. Animal dark bluish gray, striped like a
zebra on each side, and irregularly mottled behind.

Habitat.—Woods and fields.

ZONITES NITIDULUS, DRAPARNAUD.

SHELL flattened, subpellucid, dull waxy-coloured above,
paler below, and clouded with opaque white round the
umbilicus; whorls four to five, convex, marked with
irregularly placed striæ, which are interrupted by the
sutures, and not continued from whorl to whorl; suture
deepish; spire slightly produced, with a blunt apex;
aperture semilunar, a little oblique; peristome not reflected; umbilicus large, exposing the second whorl.
Diameter $\frac{3}{8}$ths to $\frac{7}{10}$ths inch. Animal dark lead coloured,
marked with tubercles of a darker colour.

Habitat.—Under stones on hedge-sides, among moss,
in woods and old walls.

v. **nitens** (*Mich.*) : Shell rather smaller, and of a lighter
colour, with a dull and waxy appearance; last whorl
somewhat larger in proportion to the others, and laterally
expanded. (= *Helix nitens*, Michaud. *Compl. Drap.*, p.
44, pl. xv., f. 1-5.)

v. **Helmii** (*Alder*): Shell pearl-white in colour.
(= *Helix Helmii*, Gilbertson's M.S.)

ZONITES PURUS, ALDER.

SHELL depressed, transparent, glossy, whitish or light
horn-coloured, with numerous transverse circular striæ;

whorls four, convex, the body-whorl occupying nearly one-half of the shell; spire not much raised, obtuse; sutures deep, narrow; aperture roundish, oblique; umbilicus narrow, deep, disclosing all the internal spire. Diam. $\frac{1}{10}$ to $\frac{1}{4}$ inch. Animal yellowish-grey, tinged with slate colour, and mottled with minute black specks.

Habitat.—Under stones and decayed leaves, in woods and fields.

v. **margaritacea** (*Jeff.*): Shell pearl-white, nearly transparent. (B. C. vol i., p. 165).

ZONITES RADIATULUS, ALDER.

SHELL flattened, shining, transparent, regularly striated, horn-coloured; whorls four to four and a half, convex, with the body-whorl large in proportion to the rest, and the striæ extending from whorl to whorl, and not interrupted by the sutures as in Z. nitidulus; spire much depressed, obtuse; suture not very deep; aperture semilunar, oblique; umbilicus moderately deep. Diameter $\frac{1}{12}$ to $\frac{1}{8}$ inch. Animal dark-brown, marked with rounded tubercles, between which are placed a few white specks.

Habitat.—Among moss and wet grass, in woods and fields.

v. **viridescenti-alba** (*Jeff.*) : Shell greenish-white. (Ferussac described a greenish-white variety of this species in his Prodromus as *Helix vitrina*, which seems to be identical with v. *viridescenti-alba* of Jeffreys).

ZONITES NITIDUS, MULLER.

SHELL depressed, subglobular, glossy, semi-transparent, transversely striated, brownish horn-coloured ; whorls five, body-whorl occupying one-half of the shell; spire produced, blunt; aperture oblique, roundish, forming

three-fourths of a circle; outer lip somewhat oblique; umbilicus narrow, deep. Diameter $\frac{3}{12}$ths inch; length half-breadth. Animal bluish-black, with thick tentacles.
Habitat.—Marshes, and banks of streams, ditches, &c.
v. albinos (*Moq.*): Shell whitish, unicolour.

ZONITES EXCAVATUS, BEAN.

SHELL depressed, thin, sub-orbicular, shining, darkish horn-coloured; striæ well-defined; whorls five and a half, convex; spire slightly produced; aperture small, lunate; umbilicus large, deep, disclosing all the whorls. Diam. maj. $6\frac{1}{4}$, min. $5\frac{3}{4}$, alt. $2\frac{3}{4}$ mill. Animal lead-coloured, with the mantle closely spotted with milk-white.
Habitat.—Woods, among moss and dead leaves.
v. vitrina (*Fér.*): Shell greenish-white, transparent.
(=*Helix vitrina*, Fér, *Tabl. Syst.* p. 45.—*H. viridula*, Menke. *Syn. Moll.*, p. 20).

ZONITES CRYSTALLINUS, MÜLLER.

SHELL nearly flat, vitreous, diaphanous, glabrous, shining; whorls four and a half to five, the body-whorl being scarcely smaller than the preceding whorl; sutures well-defined, shallow; aperture lunate; umbilicus small. Diam. maj. 4, min. $3\frac{1}{2}$, alt. $1\frac{3}{4}$ mill. Animal milk-white with inky-black dorsal, and greyish ventral tentacles.
Habitat.—Woods and hedgerows, among moss and decaying leaves.
v. complanata (*Jeff.*): Shell nearly flat on both sides, the last whorl proportionately larger than the others. (B. C. vol. 1., p. 170).

ZONITES FULVUS, MÜLLER.

SHELL conical, smooth, glossy, dark horn-coloured, semi-transparent; whorls five and a half to six; periphery bluntly carinated; spire produced, blunt; aperture crescent-shaped, narrow; umbilicus shallow, not very distinct.

Habitat.—Woods and hedgerows, among stones and decaying leaves.

v. Mortonii (*Jeff.*): Shell depressed above, less flattened below, peripheral keel sharper. (=*Helix Mortonii*, Jeffr. *Linn. Trans.* vol. xvi., p. 332).

v. Alderi (*Gray*) : Shell smaller, darker brown in colour. (Alder, *Mag. Z and B.* ii., 108).

v. viridula (*Taylor*) : Shell transparent, greenish-white.

HELIX LAMELLATA, JEFF.

SHELL conoid, globose, thin, transparent, yellowish horn-colour; epidermis raised into numerous close-set plaits; whorls six, convex; spire slightly depressed, blunt; suture deep; aperture crescent-shaped; umbilicus small, very deep. Diam. $2\frac{1}{3}$, alt. 2 mill. Animal yellowish-white, with the back of a slaty-grey and a mid-dorsal yellowish-white line.

Habitat.—Woods and groves.

HELIX ACULEATA, MÜLLER.

SHELL very small, conical, globose, brownish horn-coloured; epidermis raised into numerous plaits, which in the middle of each whorl become produced into spinous points; whorls four to four and a half, convex; aperture nearly semi-circular; umbilicus small. Diam. $2\frac{1}{2}$, alt. $2\frac{3}{4}$ mill. Body varying in colour from slaty to pale-brown.

Habitat.—Woods and hedgerows, among moss and decaying leaves.

v. albida (*Jeff.*): Shell of a whitish colour. (B. C. vol. 1., p. 176).

HELIX POMATIA, LINN.

SHELL very large, globose, ventricose, obliquely striated, strong, whitish-yellow, banded with pale brown; whorls four to five, the body-whorl occupying two-thirds of the shell; spire short, blunt; aperture roundish, lunate; inner lip reflected; umbilicus very narrow. Diam. maj.

47, min. 39, alt. 39 mill. Animal warty, varying in colour from yellowish-grey to pale brown; mantle trilobed. *Habitat.*—Woods and hedgerows in chalky districts.

Fig. 13.—*Helix Pomatia.*

v. albida (*Moq.*): Shell whitish, unicolour.
v. sinistralis (*Paëtel*): Spire reversed.

HELIX ASPERSA, MÜLLER.

Shell conoid, globose, wrinkled, yellowish-brown, marked with darker bands which are interrupted at intervals by white or yellowish streaks; whorls four to four and a half, convex, the body whorl being proportionally large; spire short, blunt; aperture oval, lunate: peristome reflected; umbilicus indistinct. Diam. maj. 41, min. 32, alt. 32 mill. Animal dark brown with white specks.

Habitat.—Woods, gardens, and fields.

v. conoidea (*Picard*): Shell an elongated cone, thin, fragile; mouth small. (= var *b*, Picard. *Moll. Somme*, 1840, p. 181).

v. globosa (*Moq.*): Shell larger, nearly globular.

v. undulata (*Moq.*): Shell smaller, very thin, transparent, reddish, with brown and whitish longitudinal, undulatory wrinklings.

v. **tenuior** (*Shuttlew*): Shell smaller, very thin, transparent, reddish, unicolor. (*Moll. Corse* in *Mittheil nat. Gesellsch, Bern.* 1843, p. 17).

v. **nigrescens** (*Moq.*): Shell blackish or of a very smoky brown-black, nearly unicolour.

v. **grisea** (*Moq.*): Shell tawny or greyish, with extremely pale bands.

v. **albescens** (*Picard*): Shell whitish, banded with reddish, or marked with flame-shaped markings of the same colour.

v. **unicolor** (*Moq.*): Shell light tawny, unicolor.

v. **flammea** (*Picard*): Shell reddish, without distinct bands, but with longitudinal flame-shaped markings, more or less interrupted. (= *var. d. rufescens*, 1. *flammea*, Picard).

v. **obscurata** (*Moq.*) : Shell reddish, with some large pale brown bands that are more or less confused in the ground colour.

v. **zonata** (*Moq.*): Shell reddish or pale yellowish, with five narrow bands, of which the three upper ones are continuous. (= *var d. rufescens*, 2. *fasciatus*. Picard. *var. quinque fasciata*, Reg! *Cat.* 1848, p. 43).

v. **virescens** (*Moq.*): Shell greenish-yellow, unicolor. (= *var. virescens concolor*. Reg! *loc. cit*).

v. **exalbida** (*Menke*): Shell yellowish or whitish, unicolor.

v. **semifusca** (*T. D. A. Cockerell*): Shell with a band formula of (123) 45, and with all the space between the suture, and the situation of the third whorl covered with chocolate-brown.

v. **lutescens** (*T. D. A. Cockerell*) : Shell yellow, with pale red-brown bands; lip white.

v. **albofasciata** (*Jeff.*) : Shell reddish-brown, with a single white band. (B. C. vol. i., p. 181).

v. minor (*Moq.*): Shell smaller.

v. maxima (*Taylor*): Shell larger.   Diam. maj. 48, min. 32, alt. 38 mill.

m. scalariforme (*Taylor*) : Spire produced, and whorls disunited. (*Vide fig.* 14.)

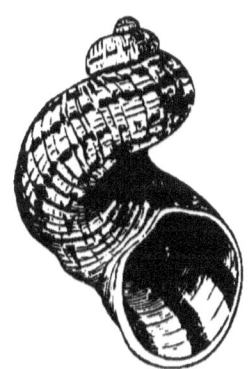

FIG. 14.—*Helix aspersa.* m. *scalariforme.*

m. sinistrorsum (*Taylor*): Spire reversed.

[To express the different modes of banding in this and the two following species as shortly as possible several formulæ —known as band-formulæ—have been adopted by conchologists. The type of each species has five bands, which are represented by the figures 12345—the 123 referring to three bands above the periphery and the 45 to two bands below it. When a band is interrupted it is shown by a colon, thus 12: 45; when slightly developed, by the insertion of the figure representing that band below the line of the others, as 12345; when obsolete by a cypher, as 02345, or 00000; and when two or more bands are confused together into one band it is shown by bracketing the figures standing for the component bands, thus 123(45), (123)(45). If more than five bands be present the extra band is represented by the insertion of the letter x into the formula, as in 12x345 or 1x2345 .

HELIX NEMORALIS, LINN.

SHELL subglobose, striated, banded or unicolor; whorls five to five and a half, convex; spire short, blunt; aperture rounded, semilunar; outer lip strong, reddish-brown; inner lip thin, reddish-brown or chocolate coloured; umbilicus indistinct. Diam. maj. 25, min. 24, alt. 15 mill. Animal dark-brown, marked with closely-set tubercles.

Habitat.—Woods, hedgerows, and gardens.

v. albescens (*Moq.*): Shell whitish.

v. Studeria (*Moq.*): Shell lilac.

v. rubella (*Moq.*): Shell pink.

v. castanea (*Moq.*): Shell brown.

v. olivacea (*Gassies*): Shell olive-brown.

v. Petiveria (*Moq.*): Shell fauve.

v. libellula (*Risso*): Shell yellow.

v. aurantia (*T. D. A. Cockerell*): Shell orange-coloured.

v. hyalozonata (*Taylor*) : Shell with transparent bands.

v. roseolabiata (*Taylor*): Peristome and rib pink or pale-brown.

v. albolabiata (*Von. Martens*): Shell with mouth and rib white.

v. interrupta (*Moq.*): Shell with the bands interrupted.

v. bimarginata (*Moq.*) : Shell with the peristome brown exteriorily, and white interiorily.

v. lurida (*Moq.*): Shell with half-effaced bands.

v. compressa (*Terver*) : Shell with the spire depressed.

v. conoidea (*Jenner*): Shell with the spire shaped like an elevated cone. Diam. 22-18 mm.

v. ponderosa (*Malm.*): Shell very thick, heavy, large; yellowish-white underneath, umbilicus often large.

v. major (*Fér.*): Shell very large.

v. minor (*Moq.*): Shell small.

m. sinistrorsum (*Westrl.*) : Shell with spire reversed.

m. scalariforme (*Taylor*): [Shell with whorls separated.

[Sheppard has divided the banded varieties into two groups, the one-banded (v. cincta), and the five banded (v. fasciata).]

HELIX HORTENSIS, MÜLLER.

SHELL closely resembling that of H. nemoralis, but smaller, thinner, and possessing a white or rose-coloured peristome.

Habitat.—Woods, hedge-banks, and gardens.

v. minor (*Moq.*): Shell dwarfed.

v. roseolabiata (*Taylor*): Shell with pink or rose-coloured rib.

v. fuscolabiata (*von Martens*): Shell with a dark peristome and rib.

v. albina (*Moq.*) : Shell whitish or white, bandless (= *v. subalbida*. Locard.)

v. coalita (*Moq.*): Shell with some, or all, of the bands united together.

v. incarnata (*Moq.*): Shell of a bright rose-colour.

v. lurida (*Moq.*): Shell with the bands demi-effaced.

v. roseozonata (*T. D. A. Cockerell*): Shell straw-colour with red-brown bands.

v. olivacea (*Taylor*) : Shell deep olive-brown.

v. lilacina (*Taylor*): Shell bluish-violet in colour.

v. arenicola (*Macgill*) : Shell with transparent, colourless bands.

v. lutea (*Moq.*): Shell yellow.

v. unicolor (*Pasc.*): Shell without bands, yellow, rose, tawny, whitish or white.

m. sinistrorsum (*Taylor*): Spire reversed.

HELIX ARBUSTORUM, LINN.

SHELL globose, thin, marked concentrically with very minute striæ, brown, marked with yellowish spots and a single blackish band, which girdles the middle of each whorl; whorls five to six, convex, the last whorl making two-thirds of the shell; spire short, conoid, obtuse; aperture rounded, lunate; peristome white, reflected. Diam. maj. 24, min. 20, alt. 16 mill. Animal dark olive-green or bluish-black, coarsely tuberculated.

Habitat.—Woods, hedgerows, and among the willows and reeds of river banks and ditch sides.

v. **Baylei** (*Lecoq*): Shell smaller, more conoid, extremely thin, very transparent, light greenish-yellow in colour.

v. **alpestris** (*Zgl.*): Shell half the usual size, spire more raised. Diam. maj. 18, min. 15, alt. 12 mill.

v. **conoidea** (*Westrl*): Shell large, conical, irregularly striate, with transverse, somewhat confluent, pale yellow markings, subperforate. Diam. 24, alt. 26 mill.

v. **fusca** (*Fér.*) : Shell very thin, subtransparent, brown, nearly unicolour.

v. **Repellina** (*Charp*) : Shell more flattened, thin, transparent, pale.

v. **marmorata** (*Roffr*) : Shell similar to type, but destitute of bands.

v. **pallida** (*Taylor*): Shell yellow, or whitish-yellow, with bands.

v. **flavescens** (*Moq.*) : Shell yellowish, nearly unicolor.

v. **albinos** (*Moq.*): Shell whitish, spotless.

m. **sinistrorsum** (*Fér.*): Shell reversed.

HELIX CANTIANA, MONT.

SHELL depressed, subglobose, thin, pellucid, yellowish-horn coloured, tinged with rose towards the aperture, and

generally marked with a faint white line near the periphery; whorls six to seven, convex, the body-whorl comprising nearly one-half of the shell; spire short, blunt;
suture rather deep; aperture lunate, slightly reflected and
marked with a white or rose-coloured rib; umbilicus
small, narrow, deep. Diam. maj. 21, min. 18, alt. 13-14
mill. Animal pale yellowish, covered with greyish tubercles.

Habitat.—On nettles and in marshy places in the
Southern Counties.

v. **albida** (*Taylor*): Shell entirely opaque white.

v. **Galloprovincialis** (*Dup.*) : Shell with the last
whorl less depressed, striæ finer and more equal, lighter in
colour; umbilicus narrower; peristome white interiorily,
reddish exteriorily. (=*Helix Galloprovincialis*, Dup.,
Hist. Moll. ii., 1848, p. 204).

v. **minor** (*Moq.*) : Shell as in preceding var., but
smaller.

v. **rubescens** (*Moq.*): Shell as in var. Galloprovincialis, but with the last whorl reddish.

v. **pyramidata** (*Colb.*) : Shell smaller, spire more
raised, pyramidal.

HELIX CARTUSIANA, MÜLLER.

SHELL depressed, globose, subpellucid, minutely striated :
whitish horn-colour marked with a milk-white spiral band
just above the periphery, not so glossy as in H. cantiana :
whorls six to seven, the body-whorl comprising nearly one
half of the shell; spire acute, more depressed than in H.
cantiana; suture deepish; aperture lunate with a white
internal rib; umbilicus minute. Diam. maj. 14; min. 11 :
alt. 7½ mill. Animal yellowish, closely tuberculated, each
tubercle being dotted with brown.

I

Habitat.—Among grass on the Kent and Surrey Downs.

v. leucoloma (*Stabile*): Shell small with white peristome and rib.

v. rufilabris (*Jeff.*): Shell smaller with the inside rib of a reddish colour. (Westerlund in his " Fauna Europa " describes this var. as " testa-globoso-depressa, polita, anfr. sat lente accrescentes, apert. rotundato-lunata, anguste sed alte rufescenti labiata, margine intus rufo-brunneo; d. 8-10, a. 6-8 mm.)

HELIX RUFESCENS, PENNANT.

SHELL depressed, subglobose, subcarinated, varying in colour from ashy-grey to rufous brown, and generally with a white band at the periphery; whorls six to seven, convex, the body-whorl comprising about one-half of the shell; spire short, blunt; aperture semi-elliptical, oblique, with a white internal rib; umbilicus narrow, distinct. Diam. maj. 14; min. 10; alt. 6 mill. Animal dusky ash-coloured, with well pronounced tubercles; dorsal tentacles long, slender; ventral tentacles short.

Habitat.—Under stones and logs of wood in woods, gardens, and hedge-banks.

v. rubens (*Moq.*): Shell more or less reddish. (= var. 4. Bouch. *Moll. Pas-de-Cal.* p. 46.)

v. alba (*Moq.*): Shell entirely white (= var. 1. Bouch. *loc. cit.*)

v. minor (*Jeff.*): Shell smaller; spire more raised. (= B. C. vol. 1. p. 195.)

HELIX CONCINNA, JEFF.

CLOSELY allied to Helix hispida, from which it may be distinguished by the following characters:—Shell larger,

less globose, hairs more liable to fall off, and in consequence the shell often appears glabrous; umbilicus wider. Animal reddish-brown, minutely tuberculated; foot narrow.

Habitat.—Under stones, among 'nettles and *Arum maculatum,* as well as at the roots of grass in moist places.

v. **minor** (*Jeff.*): Shell smaller and white; spire more depressed than usual. (B. C. vol. 1, p. 197.)

v. **albida** (*Jeff.*): Shell white. (B. C. vol. 1., p. 197.)

HELIX HISPIDA, LINN.

S HELL depressed, suborbiculate, thin, semitransparent, transversely striated, yellowish-brown, epidermis covered with fine white recurved hairs; whorls six to seven, convex, the body-whorl comprising one-third of the shell; spire somewhat raised, blunt; aperture semilunar, oblique, sometimes provided with an internal rib; umbilicus small, narrow, deep. Diam. maj. 10; min. 9; alt. 5½ mill. Animal greyish-brown or slate-colour, mottled with black tubercles speckled with milk-white; foot thick, yellowish-white.

Habitat.—Among moss, grass, and under stones in shady places.

v. **subrufa** (*Moq.*): Shell thicker, reddish, glabrous. (= v. β. Drap. *Hist. Moll.* 1805, p. 104—var. *a minor*, Picard, *Moll. Somme,* 1840, p. 228.)

v. **fusca** (*Menke*): Shell light brown in colour.

v. **nana** (*Jeff.*): Shell much smaller but with a strong labial rib; spire depressed. (B. C. vol. 1, p. 199.)

v. **subglobosa** (*Jeff.*): Shell more globular, and much thinner, horn-colour or white; umbilicus very small. (B. C. vol. 1, p. 199.)

I 2

v. depilata (*Alder*): Shell usually more depressed, glabrous; whorls more round; peristome more thickened; columella more angulated.

v. conica (*Jeff.*) : Shell smaller, spire more raised. (B. C. vol i., p. 199.)

v. albida (*Jeff.*): Shell white or colourless, thinner. (B. C., vol i., p. 199.)

HELIX SERICEA, MÜLLER.

SHELL subglobular, conical, thin, pellucid, dark-brown or greyish-white, marked with a few faintly marked reddish-brown streaks; epidermis covered with fine, long, downy hairs, which, when broken off, give the shell a granulated appearance; whorls six, very convex, the body-whorl comprising nearly one-half of the shell; spire much raised, obtuse; aperture crescent-shaped, provided with a small, internal, white rib; umbilicus very small, deep. Diam. maj. 16; min. 14½; alt. 9½ mill. Animal yellowish-grey; mantle reddish-brown, spotted with milk-white.

Habitat.—Woods and damp places.

v. cornea (*Jeff.*) : Shell horn-colour, very thin, glossy and semi-transparent; labial rib perceptible on the outside. (B. C. vol. i., p. 201.)

v. carinata (*Taylor*): Shell sharply angled at the periphery; aperture diam. 4 mill.; alt. 2½ mill.

v. albida : Shell white or whitish.

HELIX RELEVATA, MICH.

SHELL depressed, subglobose, orbicular, thin, diaphanous, glossy, greenish horn-coloured, hispid, striated and corrugated; whorls four and a half, convex, ventricose, the body-whorl comprising two-thirds of the shell; spire

very slightly produced, blunt; suture very deep; aperture nearly circular, not provided with a rib; umbilicus small, narrow, moderately shallow. Diam. maj. 7; min. 6; alt. 5 mill. Animal yellowish-grey; mantle yellowish-brown, speckled with brown and milk-white.

Habitat.—Among nettles in shady places.

HELIX FUSCA, MONTAGU.

SHELL subconical, depressed, very thin, fragile, pellucid, glabrous, glossy, horn-coloured, marked with strongly developed, irregular, transverse wrinkles; whorls five to five and a half, convex, the body-whorl comprising slightly more than half of the shell; spire somewhat produced, blunt; suture shallow; aperture lunate; outer lip reflected over the umbilicus; umbilicus very narrow. Diam. maj. 9; min. 7; alt. 5 mill. Animal yellowish-grey, speckled with black.

Habitat.—On the under sides of the leaves of sycamores and alders, among decayed leaves in woods.

HELIX PISANA, MÜLLER.

SHELL subglobose, yellowish-white, marked with chocolate brown bands and dots of the same colour, so as to give the shell a mottled appearance; whorls five to five and a half, convex, the body-whorl comprising about two-thirds of the shell; spire somewhat produced, blunt; aperture lunate, dilated, forming three-fourths of a circle; peristome reflected; umbilicus small, oblique. Diam. maj. 20; min. 18; alt. 14 mill. Animal yellowish-grey, tinged with reddish.

Habitat.—Sandhills near the coast.

v. lineolata (*Moq.*): Shell whitish, with numerous fine brown or red lines, above and below.

v. **alba** (*Shuttl.*): Shell white or pale yellow in colour.

HELIX VIRGATA, DA COSTA.

SHELL somewhat globular, conical, white or cream-colour, marked with a single dark-brown band in the middle of the body-whorl, and with several bands beneath ; whorls six, convex, the body-whorl comprising more than one-half of the shell; spire sub-elevated, apex brownish ; aperture purplish-brown, rounded, ovate ; umbilicus narrow, deep. Diam. maj. 19; min. 17; alt. 12 mill. Animal pink or yellowish white; tentacles dark grey.

Habitat.—Sandhills near the coast.

v. **albicans** (*Gratel*): Shell entirely white or whitish, without markings.

v. **rufula** (*Moq.*): Shell deep red.

v. **bifasciata** (*Bouch.*): Shell white, with two brown continuous bands above, and several bands, more or less entire, below.

v. **leucozona** (*Taylor*): Shell violet-brown or reddish-brown, with a white zone at the periphery, and sometimes with a paler area around the umbilicus.

v. **ochroleuca** (*Moq.*): Shell white, with a large yellow band above, and several semi-effaced bands below.

v. **nigrescens** (*Gratel*): Shell with some bands and spots of a black-brown colour (= *var.* 5. *nigrescens*, Gratel. *Moll. Land.* 1829.)

v. **tessellata** (*Bouch.*): Shell with some interrupted bands above and below.

v. **lutescens** (*Moq.*): Shell entirely yellowish.

v. **pelluscens** (*Shuttl.*): Shell extremely thin, sub-transparent (= *Helix pelluscens*, Shuttlew ; in *Coll. Blaim. Reg. Cat.*, 1848, p. 313.)

v. **hypozonata** (*Moq.*): Shell white, unicolor above, with several bands below.

v. **submaritima** (*Des Moul.*): Shell smaller, slightly pyramidal, darker in colour. (= var. *e. submaritima*, Des Moul., *Moll Gir, Suppl. in Bull. Soc. Linn. Bord.*, 1829, p. 16.)

v. **subalbida** (*Poiret*): Shell white, with one continuous band above, unicolorous below. (= *Helix subalbida*, Poir, *Podr.*, p. 83.)

v. **subaperta** (*Jeff.*): Shell of a whitish hue; spire more depressed; umbilicus wider. (B. C. vol. i., p. 210.)

v. **subglobosa** (*Jeff.*): Shell smaller, with a double band above the periphery, last whorl larger in proportion to the others; umbilicus wider. (B. C. vol. i., p. 210.)

v. **carinata** (*Jeff.*): Shell yellowish-white, compressed above; periphery strongly keeled. (B. C. vol. i., p. 210.)

v. **alba** (*Taylor*): Shell white.

v. **major** (*Taylor*): Shell larger. Diam. 20 mill.

v. **minor** (*Taylor*): Shell smaller. Diam. 6½ mill.

m. **sinistrorsum** (*Taylor*): Spire reversed.

HELIX CAPERATA, MONTAGU.

HELL depressed, subconical, marked with numerous rib-like striæ, which run concentrically, whitish or dull yellowish-white, banded with brown; whorls six; periphery bluntly carinated; spire slightly produced, apex tipped with black or brown; suture rather deep; aperture rounded, lunate, marked with a strong white rib; umbilicus large, deep. Diam. maj. 11; min. 9⅔; alt. 7 mill. Body ash-colour, streaked with brown, tuberculated.

Habitat.—Under stones and among herbage in dry places.

v. **obliterata** (*Picard*): Shell white, with transverse markings.

v. **alba** (*Picard*): Shell pure white, without markings.

v. fulva (*Moq.*) : Shell dark brown or brownish, with some transverse whitish lines.

v. bizonalis (*Moq.*) : Shell whitish, with two continuous bands above, and several below.

v. ornata (*Picard*) : Shell smaller, whitish, with one brown continuous band above, and two to six below. (= var. *c.*, *ornata*, Picard, *Moll Somme.*, 1840, p. 230).

v. Gigaxii (*Charp.*); Shell smaller, more depressed, reddish, spotted above, and marked by two bands below.

v. subscalaris (*Jeff.*) : Shell conical, whorls more convex. (B. C. vol. i., p. 214).

v. major ((*Jeff.*) : Shell larger. (B. C. vol. i., p. 214).

HELIX ERICETORUM, MÜLLER.

Shell depressed, circular, semitransparent, greyish or whitish, banded with chestnut brown ; whorls six ; spire slightly produced, apex obtuse, brown ; suture deepish ; periphery not keeled ; aperture nearly circular ; umbilicus large, open, exposing three or four whorls. Diam. maj. 17 ; min. 14½ ; alt. 8 mill. Animal reddish-brown or yellowish-grey, with colourless tubercles.

Habitat.—Dry heaths and downs ; chalky districts near the sea.

v. lutescens (*Moq.*) : Shell dirty-yellowish, unicolour.

v. leucozona (*Moq.*) : Shell reddish, with one white line on the last whorl, and often several white and brown lines below.

v. alba (*Charp.*) : Shell entirely white.

v. major (*Locard*) : Shell large ; diam. 20-10 mill.

v. minor (*Moq.*) : Shell smaller.

v. instabilis (*Ziegl.*) : Shell smaller, or a darker colour, and sometimes streaked or spotted ; spire more raised ; umbilicus narrower (= *H. instabilis*, Ziegler.) B. C. vol. i., p. 217.

m. disjunctum (*Turton*) : Whorls disjointed.

m. sinistrorsum (*Jeff.*): Spire reversed. (B. C. vol. i., p. 217.)

HELIX ROTUNDATA, MÜLLER.

SHELL depressed, circular, thin, yellowish or reddish-grey, marked with brown and yellowish-grey spots, which radiate from the centre; whorls six to seven; spire slightly produced, with a glossy apex; suture deepish; periphery bluntly carinated; aperture semi-lunar, thin, not reflected, with a white internal rib in old specimens; umbilicus large, deep, exposing all the whorls. Diam. maj. 8; min. 7⅓; alt. 3 mill. Animal slaty-grey, spotted with black.

Habitat.—In decaying wood, among fallen leaves, under stones. Very common.

v. **rufula** (*Moq.*): Shell tawny, spotless.

v. **Turtonii** (*Flem.*): Shell almost flat above. (= *Helix rotundata.* Turt., *Dict.*, 1819, p. 53.—*H. rotundata, var* β., Turt. *Shells, Brit.*, 1831, p. 59.)

v, **alba** (*Moq.*): Shell entirely whitish or nearly so, spotless, transparent.

v. **pyramidalis** (*Jeff.*): Shell sub-conical; spire more raised. (B. C. vol. i., p. 219).

v. **minor** (*Jeff.*): Shell smaller. (B. C. vol. i., p. 219).

HELIX RUPESTRIS, DRAPARNAUD.

SHELL depressed below, sub-conical, slightly glossy, with strong, oblique, transverse striæ, blackish-brown; whorls five; spire somewhat produced, apex smooth; suture deep; aperture nearly circular; umbilicus very large, deep. Diam. maj. 3¼; min. 3; alt. 2½ mill. Animal dark slaty-grey or dusky-red.

Habitat.—Between the bricks in old walls and castle ruins, calcareous soils.

v. viridescenti-alba (*Jeff.*): Shell greenish-white. (B. C. vol. i., p. 221.)

HELIX PYGMÆA, DRAPARNAUD.

SHELL very minute, nearly circular, depressed, thin, pale brown horn-colour ; whorls four ; spire somewhat produced, apex glossy ; suture deep ; aperture semi-lunar : umbilicus large, deep. Diam. maj. 1⅔ ; min. 1½ ; alt. ¾ mill. Animal slaty-grey or darkish-brown, speckled with black.

Habitat.—Among dead leaves, under stones, and at the roots of grass. Moderately common.

HELIX PULCHELLA, MÜLLER.

SHELL sub-depressed, milk-white, glossy, semi-transparent, convex equally above and below ; whorls three and a half, the body-whorl exceeding in size the rest of the shell ; spire slightly produced ; suture rather deep ; aperture circular ; peristome very thick, reflected so as to form a double peristome ; umbilicus large, deep. Diam. maj. 3 ; min. 2½ ; alt. 1½ mill. Animal milk-white ; eyes black.

Habitat.—Under stones, among moss and grass in damp places.

v. costata (*Müll.*): Shell not so glossy, slightly reddish, with numerous transverse, curved, membranous ribs as well as intermediate striæ. (= *H. costata*, Mull., *Verm. Hist.* ii., 1774, p. 31).

v. lævigata (*Moq.*): Shell glossy, whitish ; peristome blunt.

HELIX LAPICIDA, LINN.

SHELL depressed, lenticular, acutely carinated at the periphery, greyish or yellowish-horn colour, streaked irregularly with rufous-brown; whorls five; spire very little produced, apex blunt, smooth; suture well defined, shallow; aperture oval, somewhat angulated above and below; outer lip whitish, reflected, and with the inner lip forming a perfect peristome; umbilicus large, deep. Diam. maj. 17; min. 15; alt. 6½ mill. Animal yellowish-brown.

Habitat.—Woods, hedge-rows, walls, and rocky places in calcareous districts.

v. **nigrescens** (*Taylor*): Shell of an uniform, very dark brownish-black, except the apex which is paler, and the peristome which is white.

v. **minor** (*Moq.*): Shell dwarfed, brown.

v. **albina** (*Menke*): Shell whitish, unicolor.

HELIX OBVOLUTA, MÜLLER.

SHELL depressed, subdiscoidal, opaque, solid, dull rufous-brown; whorls six and a half; spire depressed, sunk below the upper level of the body-whorl; suture rather deep; aperture triangular, marked with two protuberances; peristome thick, pinkish-white, much reflected; umbilicus large, deep. Diam. maj. 13; min. 12; alt. 6 mill. Animal light reddish-brown above, and pale greyish-brown below.

Habitat—Among the moss near the roots of shady trees. Rare.

BULIMUS ACUTUS, MÜLLER.

SHELL conical, turretted, irregularly striate, yellowish-white with streaks of pale brown, and sometimes a reddish-brown or blackish band below the periphery; whorls eight to nine, rounded; spire tapering, blunt; suture rather deep; aperture oval; outer lip thin, reflected; umbilicus narrow, rather shallow. Length 15; diam. 5½ mill.; ap. 5 mill. long., 3 wide. Animal light yellowish-grey.

Habitat.—Downs and dunes on the south and west coasts.

v. **elongata** (*Cr. and Jan.*): Shell more slender. (=*Bulimus elongatus*, Crist. and Jan., *Cat.* x., No. 1772.)

v. **inflata** (*Moq.*): Shell a little ventricose.

v. **bizona** (*Moq.*): Shell with the striæ obliterated, greyish or whitish, with two dark bands on the body-whorl.

v. **strigata** (*Menke*): Shell with broad whitish, or white, ribs alternating with transverse semi-translucent brownish-grey streaks.

v. **articulata** (*Lam.*): Shell with transverse white ribs, alternating with broad stripes of violet brown.

v. **nigrescens** (*Taylor*): Shell violet-brown, with a few fine, whitish, transverse striæ, and a pale area around the umbilicus.

v. **alba** (*Requien*): Shell entirely white.

BULIMUS MONTANUS, DRAPARNAUD.

SHELL oblong, conical, semi-transparent, glossy, with spiral, fine, close-set striæ, pale brownish horn-colour or a deeper brown; whorls six and a half to seven and a half, compressed, the body-whorl comprising slightly less than half the shell; spire tapering, apex blunt; suture oblique, shallow; aperture oval, pinkish or brownish internally; peristome thick, reflected over the umbilicus; umbilicus

narrow, rather deep. Length 15, diam. 6 mill. Ap.. within 5½ mill. long, 3 wide. Animal greyish-brown or dark red, speckled with black.

Habitat.—Among fallen beech leaves, and in woods of the Southern Counties.

v. albina (*Moq.*) : Shell whitish, unicolor.

BULIMUS OBSCURUS, MÜLLER.

SHELL oblong, oval, thin, glossy, semitransparent, brown ; whorls six and a half, rounded ; spire elongated, apex blunt ; suture rather deep : aperture oval ; peristome white, very much reflected ; umbilicus narrow, not deep. Length 10, diam. 4½ mill. Ap. within 3 mill. long, 2 wide. Animal pale brown or rosy-grey above, darker below ; tentacles subulate.

Habitat.—Under stones or moss in woods and on old walls.

v. albinos (*Moq.*) : Shell whitish, unicolor.

BULIMUS GOODALLII, MILLER.

SHELL subperforated, elongated, turretted, apex obtuse, thin, striated, pellucid, horn-coloured ; whorls seven to eight, scarcely convex, the body-whorl occupying one-third of the shell ; columella subtortuous ; aperture oblong, ovate ; peristome simple, acute. Length 6½, diam. 2 mill. Ap. 2 mill. long, 1 wide.

PUPA SECALE, DRAPARNAUD.

SHELL subcylindrical, conical, glossy, rufous horn-coloured, obliquely striated in line of growth; whorls eight to nine, gradually increasing; spire produced, apex blunt; suture moderately deep; aperture semi-oblong with seven or eight laminar teeth,—two or three on the columella, two on the columellar lip, and four on the outer lip; peristome slightly reflected; umbilicus small, oblique. Length 8, diam. 3 mill. Ap. 2⅔ mill. long, 2 wide. Animal reddish or brownish-grey above, slaty-grey below; mantle speckled with black.

Habitat.—Roots of trees, under stones, and in the cracks in oolite limestone.

v. minor (*Moq.*): Shell smaller.

v. edentula (*Taylor*): Peristome edentulous.

v. Boileausiana (*Charp*): Shell with the larger denticle entirely double, and with a supernumerary projecting denticle at the angle of the columellar border.

PUPA RINGENS, JEFF.

SHELL conical, subcylindrical, globose, glossy, light-brown or yellowish horn-colour; whorls six to six and a half; spire short, obtuse; suture well-defined, shallow; aperture subsemicircular, with five folds; peristome pale reddish-brown, reflected; umbilicus oblique, distinct, narrow. Length 4, diam. 2 mill. Ap. scarcely 1 mill. long. Animal yellowish-grey or slate-colour above, streaked with dark lines, white below.

Habitat.—Under stones, among moss and dead leaves in moist woods.

v. pallida (*Jeff.*): Shell of a lighter colour, sometimes whitish. (B. C. vol. i., p. 245).

PUPA UMBILICATA, DRAPARNAUD.

SHELL oblong, cylindrical, glabrous, glossy, diaphanous, yellowish-brown or dark horn-colour; whorls six to seven, rounded; spire short, blunt; suture shallow, oblique; aperture obliquely semi-oval, with a single denticle at the angle formed by the junction of the outer lip; outer lip broad, much reflected, white, yellowish-grey, pink or reddish-brown internally; umbilicus small, narrow. Length 4, diam. 2 mill. Ap. 1¾ mill. long. Animal greyish-brown, with the head and tentacles spotted with black.

Habitat.—Under the bark of old trees, in clefts of rocks, and old walls, under stones, and among decayed leaves.

v. edentula (*Moq.*): Peristome of the shell without denticles. (=*Pupa umbilicata, var. b*, Turton. *Shells Brit.*, p. 98).

v. Sempronii (*Charp.*): Shell small, aperture without denticle, lip not white.

v. curta (*Pasc.*): Shell shorter, ovoidal, tumid.

v. albina (*Moq.*): Shell entirely white.

PUPA MARGINATA, DRAPARNAUD.

SHELL ovate, cylindrical, glabrous, finely striated, yellowish-horn or light brown in colour; whorls six to seven, convex, slightly compressed; spire short, apex blunt; suture rather deep; aperture subsemicircular, provided with a small denticle, which is placed in the middle of the base of· the last whorl, and with a strong, white external rib behind the outer lip; umbilicus narrow. Length 3½; diam. scarcely 2 mill.; ap. 1⅓ mill. long. Animal grey-black above, paler, and covered with black specks below.

Habitat.—Under stones, among moss and dead leaves.

v. bigranata (*Rossm.*): Shell with a dentiform palatal

callosity. (= *Pupa bigranata*, Rossm. *Icongr.* ix., x.,
p. 25, fig. 645.)

v. edentula (*Moq.*): Shell edentulous.

v. albina (*Menke*): Shell whitish, unicolor.

v. brevis (*Baud*); Shell very short, robust, callosity
thick, peristome white.

VERTIGO ANTIVERTIGO, DRAPARNAUD.

Shell dextral, oval, ventricose, shining, chestnut-brown coloured; whorls four and a half, the body whorl comprising about one-half of the shell; spire short, apex blunt; suture rather deep; aperture oblique, subcordate, provided with from six to eight teeth; outer lip reflected, strengthened by a rib; umbilicus distinct, narrow. Length $2\frac{1}{3}$; diam. almost $1\frac{1}{2}$ mill.; ap. $\frac{2}{3}$ mill. long. Body greyish-black.

Habitat.—In marshy places, under stones on the banks of streams and rivers.

v. **sexdentata** (*Mont.*): Aperture with six denticles.

v. **octodentata** (*Hartm. Stud.*): Peristome with eight denticles.

VERTIGO LILLJEBORGI, WESTERLUND.

Shell oval, thin, light yellowish horn-colour; whorls four and a half, globose, the body-whorl being larger than the rest of the shell; spire short, apex very obtuse; suture exceedingly deep; aperture semi-oval, with from four to five denticles—two on the outer lip, one on the collumellar lip, and one on the middle of the columella; outer lip thin, reflected, with a white external rib; inner lip indistinct; umbilicus open. Length $2-2\frac{1}{4}$; diam. $1-1\frac{1}{4}$ mill. Animal dark-grey above, paler below.

Rare.

v. **bidentata** (*Jeff.*): Labial or palatal teeth wanting. (B. C. vol. i., p. 256.)

VERTIGO MOULINSIANA, DUP. NON JEFF.

Shell differing from that of V. Lilljeborgi, in being more swollen and barrel-shaped, and in having the labial rib much stouter:

Rare.

VERTIGO TUMIDA, WESTERLUND.

SHELL ovate, ventricose, dark reddish-yellow or reddish-brown; spire conical above, short, blunt; whorls four and a half to five, convex; aperture wide, inequally cordate, with six denticles—two parietal, two columellar, and two palatal; between the columellar and palatal denticles are two tubercles; outer margin of peristome simple, thin, strong above, and greatly curved. Length $1\frac{7}{8}$; diam. $1\frac{1}{4}$ mill.

Rare.

VERTIGO PYGMÆA, DRAPARNAUD.

SHELL dextral, ovate, cylindrical, rather ventricose, faintly striate, reddish-brown; whorls four and a half to five, rounded, body-whorl comprising about one-half of the shell; spire short, blunt; suture well-marked; aperture semi-oval, with four or five teeth—one on the columella, two or three on the internal side of the outer lip, and one in the middle of the base of the penultimate whorl; umbilicus narrow, rather deep. Length $2\frac{1}{2}$: diam. $2\frac{1}{3}$ mill.; ap. $\frac{2}{3}$ mill. long. Animal slaty-grey.

Habitat.—Under stones, logs of wood, and at the roots of grass.

v. quadridenta (*Stud.*): Shell with only two palatal plications.

v. pallida (*Jeff.*): Shell thinner, lighter in colour. (B. C. vol. i., p. 258.)

VERTIGO ALPESTRIS, ALDER.

SHELL differing from that of V. pygmæa in being more cylindrical, lighter in colour, and in the absence of any rib. The tentacles and the foot are longer than in V. pygmæa.

Habitat.—Among grass and dead leaves in the Northern Counties.

VERTIGO SUBSTRIATA, JEFFREYS

SHELL shortly ovate, strongly striated, subopaque, light yellowish horn-colour; whorls four and a half, very ventricose; spire short, abrupt, blunt; suture very deep; aperture oblique, subpyriform, with six teeth; two or three inside the outer lip, two on the base of the penultimate whorl, and one, sometimes two, on the columella; umbilicus small, contracted by a basal ridge. Length 2; diam. $4\frac{1}{3}$ mill.; ap. $\frac{2}{3}$ mill. long. Animal grey; snout bilobed.

Habitat.—Among dead leaves and grass, under stones, in marshy places.

VERTIGO PUSILLA, MÜLLER.

SHELL sinistral, ovate, somewhat fusiform, glossy, thin, transparent, pale yellowish horn-colour; whorls four and a half to five, very ventricose, the last two of equal breadth; suture deep; aperture subquadrate, with a sinuation on the outer margin, and with six or seven denticles,—two inside the outer lip, two on the base of the penultimate whorl, and two or three on the columella: outer lip thickish, furnished externally and internally with a strong rib of a yellowish-white colour; umbilicus small, contracted by a basal rib. Length 2; diam. 1 mill.; ap. $\frac{3}{4}$ mill. long. Animal brownish or greyish-slate colour; mantle yellowish-brown.

Habitat.—Among moss and decaying leaves, under stones in woods, old walls and dry banks.

VERTIGO ANGUSTIOR, JEFFREYS.

SHELL sinistral, smaller and narrower than Vertigo pusilla, fusiform, glossy, semitransparent, pale fulvous; whorls four and a half, slightly ventricose; spire somewhat produced, blunt; suture deepish; aperture triangularly subcordate, with from four to five denticles,—one on the columella, two on the inside of the outer lip, and two on the base of the penultimate whorl; outer lip provided with a strong, yellowish-white rib, thick; umbilicus small, contracted by a basal ridge. Length scarcely 2; diam. hardly 1 mill.; ap. $\frac{3}{3}$ mill. long. Animal greyish, with a yellowish-grey mantle.

Habitat.—Roots of grass in marshy places.

VERTIGO EDÉNTULA, DRAPARNAUD.

SHELL dextral, ovate, cylindrical, thin, glossy, pale brown or horn-coloured, transversely [marked with faint striæ; whorls five to six and a half, gradually increasing; spire conical, blunt; suture moderately deep; aperture subsemioval, toothless; umbilicus narrow, deepish. Length $3\frac{3}{3}$; diam. $1\frac{3}{3}$ mill.; ap. $1\frac{1}{2}$ mill. long. Animal pale grey, with darker tentacles.

Habitat.—Under stones, among moss and dead leaves, in moist places and woods.

v. columella (*von Martens*): Shell somewhat longer, and having the last whorl a little broader than the next. (= *Pupa columella* (von Martens), Benz, *Ueber Würtenburg, Faun.*, p. 49.)

VERTIGO MINUTISSIMA, HARTMANN.

SHELL dextral, cylindrical, narrower and smaller than V. edentula, elegantly striated, glossy, horn-colour; whorls five and a half, rounded, increasing in size to the third, and then continuing of the same breadth; spire produced, very obtuse; suture deepish : aperture oblong, subcircular, edentulous, curved inwards towards the centre of the lower lip; umbilicus oblique, narrow. Length 2; diam. ⅔ mill.; ap. nearly ⅔ mill. long. Animal grey, spotted with black; mantle greyish-brown.

Habitat.—Under stones on hillsides.

BALIA PERVERSA, LINN.

SHELL sinistral, fusiform, turretted, transparent, glossy, yellowish horn-colour, streaked with white, irregularly striated ; whorls seven to eight, convex ; spire turretted, blunt, unstriated, polished ; suture deepish ; aperture rounded, pyriform, with sometimes a denticle near the middle of the base of the penultimate whorl; umbilical chink narrow.   Length $9\frac{1}{2}$; diam. $2\frac{2}{3}$ mill. ; ap. $2\frac{1}{3}$ mill. long, $1\frac{2}{3}$ wide.   Animal dark brown, tinged with grey.

Habitat.—Under the bark of old trees, and among the lichens growing upon them.

v. **viridula** (*Jeff.*): Shell greenish-white, transparent. (B. C. vol. i., p. 274.)

v. **simplex** (*Moq.*): Peristome without callosity, whitish.

CLAUSILIA RUGOSA, DRAPARNAUD.

SHELL cylindrical, fusiform, diaphanous, glossy, chocolate-brown or horn-coloured, marked with whitish streaks, and with closely-set, strong striæ; whorls ten to thirteen, the body-whorl slightly narrower than the two preceding it; spire tapering, blunt; suture bordered with white, oblique: aperture oval, pyriform, furnished with several plaits—two more or less prominent ones on the base of ' the penultimate whorl, with one to three smaller plaits between them, and two on the columella, one semilunar, the other small and indistinctly spiral; outer lip white, reflected, detached; basal crest sharp, angular; umbilicus narrow; clausilium oblong, oval; length 12-14; diam. hardly 3 mill. Ap. 2⅔ mill. long, 2 wide. Animal greyish-brown.

Habitat.—Under stones, on walls, and trunks of beech and ash trees.

v. dubia (*Drap.*): Shell larger, more ventricose. (= *Clausilia dubia*, Drap. *Hist.* 70, t. 4, f. 10; Alder, *Cat. Supp.* 3, *Mag. Zool and Bot.* ii., 111.)

v. Everetti (*Miller*): Shell shorter, whorls fewer. (= *Clausilia Everetti.* Miller, *Ann. Phil., n. s.* xix., 377, 1822.)

v. gracilior (*Jeff.*): Shell longer and more slender. (B. C. vol. i., p. 279.)

v. tumidula (*Jeff.*): Shell smaller, shorter, and more ventricose. (B. C. vol. i., p. 279.)

v. Schlechtii (*Zelebor*): Shell generally larger, more elongated, smoother, and more transparent than var. dubia, pale brown, frequently resembling in external appearance Clausilia laminata both in smoothness and transparency.

v. parvula (*Turton*): Shell smaller, more slender. (= *Clausilia parvula.* Leach, *MSS., B. M.*, Turton, *Zool.*

Journ. ii., 556; *Man.* ed. i., 74, f. 58; Jeffreys, *Linn. Trans.*
xvi., 352; non Studer.)

v. albinos (*Moq.*): Shell whitish.

m. dextrorsum (*Jeff.*): Shell resembling a Pupa in
shape; spire dextral. (B. C. vol. i., p. 279.)

CLAUSILIA ROLPHII, GRAY.

SHELL fusiform, glossy, thin, reddish or yellowish-brown,
closely and strong striated; whorls nine to ten, ventricose;
spire blunt; suture shallow, oblique; aperture rounded,
pyriform, sinuous on the outer side, with plaits as in C.
rugosa, but the lower one on the base of the penultimate
whorl is less prominent and sometimes cruciate; peristome
detached, thick, white; umbilicus ill-defined; clausilium
oblong. Length 13; diam. 3 mill. Ap. nearly 3 mill. long,
2 wide. Animal dark reddish-brown; mantle yellowish-
white, spotted with white.

Habitat.—Among dead leaves, under stones, and the
bark of trees in woods.

v. pellucida (*Taylor*): Shell colourless, transparent.

CLAUSILIA BIPLICATA, MONT.

SHELL fusiform, slender, diaphanous, yellowish-brown,
marked with closely-set, strong striae, some of which are
streaked with white; periphery obtusely angulated;
whorls twelve to thirteen, compressed; spire tapering,
blunt; suture oblique, shallow; aperture pyriform, canali-
culated, with the same plaits as in C. rugosa and C.
Rolphii, except that the teeth between the folds on the
base of the penultimate whorls are not represented;
peristome white, thick, detached; basal crest prominent;
clausilium oval. Length 16-17; diam. 4 mill. Ap. 4 mill.

long, 3 wide. Animal reddish-grey; foot ashy-grey, speckled with white.

Habitat.—Woods and hedges, and on the bark of willow trees.

v. **Nelsoni** (*Jeff.*): Shell rather more slender than the usual form, almost totally devoid of striation, and translucent, the axis being visible through the shell; the last whorls tinged with a very pale reddish-brown passing into whitish in the upper part.

CLAUSILIA LAMINATA, MONT.

SHELL large, fusiform, thin, highly polished, finely striated, yellowish-brown; whorls twelve, compressed; spire turretted, apex obtuse; suture oblique, shallow; aperture oval, pyriform, with two very strong plaits on the base of the penultimate whorl, and three or four labial plaits which are distinctly visible from the outside; peristome white, thick; basal crest slight; umbilicus small; clausilium with a marginal notch near its base. Length 17; diam. 4 mill. Ap. 4½ mill. long, 3 wide. Animal greyish-brown.

Habitat.—Among decayed leaves in beech woods, and on the bark of trees.

v. **pellucida** (*Jeff.*): Shell thinner, more transparent, and very glossy. (B. C. vol. i., p. 285.)

v. **albinos** (*Moq.*): Shell entirely white.

COCHLICOPA TRIDENS, PULT,

SHELL fusiform, glossy, semitransparent, transversely striated, pale yellowish-brown; periphery rounded in old, but sharply carinated in young specimens; whorls seven, the penultimate and body-whorls broader than the others; spire produced, blunt; suture shallow, fringed with a moniliform band; aperture pyriform, oblique, furnished with three or more folds—one on the columella, one in the middle of the base of the penultimate whorl, and another on the inside edge of the outer lip, while between these there are often additional denticles; peristome sinuous, strengthened by a flesh-coloured rib. Length 7; diam. 3 mill. Ap. oblique 2⅔ mill. long. Animal slaty-grey, speckled with black.

Habitat.—Among moss and decaying leaves in moist woods.

v. **Nouletiana** (*Dup.*): Shell rather larger and thinner, with a single denticle only on the outer lip.

v. **Alzenensis** (*St. Simon*): Outer lip bearing two deeply-seated denticles in addition to those described in the typical form.

v. **crystallina** (*Dup.*): Shell greenish-white, transparent, glossy.

m. **sinistrorsum** (*Taylor*): Spire reversed.

COCHLICOPA LUBRICA, MÜLLER.

SHELL oblong, ovate, glossy, transparent, smooth, yellowish-brown, or greenish-white; whorls five to five and a half, convex, body-whorl comprising about one-half of the shell; spire produced, blunt; suture rather deep with a wrinkled band; aperture oval, elliptical, without teeth or plaits; outer lip thick, strengthened by a reddish internal rib; inner lip thin. Length 6; diam. 2½ mill.

Ap. 2½ mill. long, 1½ wide. Animal slaty-grey ; mantle brownish-grey, speckled with white.

Habitat.—Among moss, decayed leaves, under stones and logs of wood

v. minor (*Fischer*) : Shell smaller.

v. lubricoides (*Fer.*) : Shell smaller, more slender.

v. ovata (*Jeff.*) : Shell much smaller and oval ; spire shorter. (B. C. vol. i., p. 293.)

v. fusca (*Moq.*) ; Shell of a more or less deep brown colour.

v. hyalina (*Jeff.*) : Shell greenish-white. (B. C. vol. i., p. 293.)

v. viridula (*Jeff.*): Shell shaped like v. lubricoides. but greenish-white. (B. C. vol. i., p. 293.)

ACHATINA ACICULA, MÜLLER.

SHELL fusiform, cylindrical, thin, very glossy, faintly striated, white; whorls five and a half to six, rapidly enlarging, body-whorl comprising about one-half of the shell; spire attenuated, obtuse; suture oblique, deep; aperture lanceolate, acutely angulated above, notched deeply at its base; outer lip flexuous; inner lip thin; umbilicus absent. Length $4\frac{2}{3}$; diam. $1\frac{1}{4}$ mill. Ap. 2 mill. long, $\frac{3}{4}$ wide. Animal white; tentacles eyeless.

Habitat.—In gravel pits, and at the roots of grass and trees.

CARYCHIUM MINIMUM, MÜLLER.

SHELL fusiform, oblong, glossy, finely striated transversely, white ; whorls five to five and a half, convex, body-whorl comprising nearly one-half of the shell ; spire with an acute apex ; suture deepish : aperture auriculate, with three denticles—one on the columella, one on the inside of the outer lip, and the third on the centre of the penulti-mate whorl ; peristome thick, reflected : umbilical chink oblique. Animal yellowish-white, bilobed in front, rounded behind.

Habitat.—Among decaying leaves and moss, under stones in moist situations.

CYCLOSTOMA ELEGANS, MÜLLER

SHELL oval, greyish or yellowish-brown, irregularly streaked and blotched with purplish-brown, ridged by numerous ribs running spirally; whorls four and a half, enlarging rapidly, tumid; spire, produced, blunt, purplish; suture very deep; aperture subrotund; umbilicus narrow, not deep; operculum shelly. Length 13-14; diam. 8½-9 mill. Animal dark-greyish brown, bilobed anteriorily; mantle speckled with milk-white on its upper part.

Habitat.—Hedgerows, margins of woods, among loose stones and moss.

v. **violacea** (*Des Mouls*): Shell violet or brown-violet, spotless, bandless, slightly transparent,

v. **purpurascens** (*Moq.*): Shell purplish, with reddish bands.

v. **ochroleuca** (*Des Mouls*): Shell yellowish, without bands or markings, rather transparent.

v. **albescens** (*Des Mouls*): Shell whitish, spotless, bandless.

v. **pallida** (*Moq.*): Shell very pale yellowish, with some spots and demi-effaced bands.

v. **marmorata** (*Brown*): Shell glabrous, unstriated.

ACME LINEATA, DRAPARNAUD.

SHELL cylindrical, attenuated, glossy, strongly striated transversely, yellowish-brown or dark-brown; whorls six to seven, compressed somewhat; apex obtusely rounded; suture shallow, well-defined; aperture roundish-oval, contracted above; outer lip thin, flexuous, reflected; inner lip thin; umbilicus minute; operculum horny. Alt. 2-3; diam. $\frac{1}{2}$-$\frac{3}{4}$ mill. Animal milk-white, speckled with brown.

Habitat.—Among decaying leaves and moss in wet situations, especially near the sea.

v. alba (*Jeff.*): Shell white or colourless, transparent. (B. C. vol. i., p. 308.)

m. sinistrorsum (*Jeff.*): Spire reversed. (B. C. vol. i., p. 308.)

GLOSSARY.

Acuminate.—Taper-pointed.
Acute.—Forming a sharp angle.
Alliaceous.—Having the smell of garlic.
Ampullaceous.—In the form of a bladder or short flask.
Angular
Angulated }.—Having angles.
Apex.—The summit of the spire.
Attenuated.—Gradually tapering to a point.
Auriculate.—Ear-shaped.

Bi-lobed.—Provided with two lobes.

Callosity.—A thickening.
Carinated.—-Provided with a keel.
Concave.—Hollow; opposed to *convex*.
Conic
Conical }.—Shaped like a cone.
Conoid
Convex.—Rounded into a nearly spherical form; opposed to *concave*.

L

CORDATE.—Heart-shaped.
CRENATED.—Scalloped.
CRUCIATE.—In the form of a cross.
CUNEATE } .—Wedge-shaped.
CUNEIFORM }
CYLINDRICAL.—Shaped like a cylinder.

DECIDUOUS.—Falling-off.
DENTATED.—Toothed.
DENTICLE.—A small tooth.
DEXIOTROPE } .—Applied to a shell with the spire turn-
DEXTRAL } ing to the right, and with the aperture
 } looking towards the left.
DIAPHANOUS.—Transparent.
DISCOID.—Disc-shaped.

EDENTULOUS.—Without teeth.
ELLIPTICAL.—Shaped like an ellipse.
EQUILATERAL.—With sides of equal length.
EQUIVALVE.—With valves of equal dimensions.
EVANESCENT.—Vanishing from notice; imperceptible.
EXCENTRIC.—Applied to the nucleus when it is not in
    the centre of the shell.

FLEXUOUS.—Bent
FUSIFORM.—Spindle-shaped.

GIBBOUS.—Swollen.
GLOBOSE.—Having, or approaching a sphæroidal form.
GLOBULAR.—Somewhat, or nearly globose.
GRANULATED.—Having numerous small elevations.

HISPID.—Hairy.

INEQUILATERAL.—With sides of unequal length.
INTORTED.—Twisted in.

LAMELLIFORM.—Shaped like a thin plate, or lamella.
LANCEOLATE.—Lance-shaped.

LAÖTROPE.—Sinistral.
LENTICULAR.—Lens-shaped.
LINEOLATE.—Marked with fine or obscure lines.
LUNATE.—Crescent-shaped.

MONILIFORM.—Necklace-shaped; beaded.
MUCRONATE.—Tipped with a short and abrupt small apex.
MULTISPIRAL.—With many spirals.

NON-OPERCULATED.—Not provided with an operculum.

OBLONG.—Considerably longer than broad, and with nearly parallel sides.
OBOVAL.—Oval, with the broader end towards the apex.
OBTUSE.—Blunt.
OPERCULATED.—Provided with an operculum.
ORBICULAR.—Flat, with a circular outline.
OVAL.—Broadly elliptical.
OVATE.—Egg-shaped.
OVOID.—Nearly oval.
OVOIDAL.—Somewhat ovoid.

PAUCISPIRAL.—With few spirals.
PECTINIFORM.—Shaped like a comb.
PELLUCID.—Transparent; diaphanous.
PENULTIMATE.—Applied to the last whorl but one.

QUADRANGULAR.—Having four angles, and, consequently, four sides.

RHOMBIC.—Shaped like a rhomb.
RHOMBOIDAL.—Shaped like a rhomboid.
ROTUND.—Rounded in outline.
RUGOSE }
RUGOUS }.—Wrinkled.

SUB.—Denotes in compounds somewhat or slightly.

SEMILUNAR.—Crescent-shaped.

SESSILE.—Destitute of a pedicle.

SETACEOUS.—Bristle-like.

SHAGREENED.—Granulated.

SINISTRAL.—Applied to a shell when the spire turns towards the left, and the aperture points to the right.

SINUATE.—With a strongly wavy or recessed margin.

SINUOUS.—Wavy.

SPHÆROIDAL.—Shaped like a sphere.

STRIATE }
STRIOLATE } .—Marked with fine lines or ridges.

SULCUS.—A groove.

TESTACEOUS.—Shelly.

TRANSLUCENT.—Not quite transparent.

TRIANGULAR.—Shaped like a triangle.

TRILOBED.—Provided with three lobes.

TROCHOID.—Wheel-shaped.

TRUNCATE.—As if cut off at the apex.

TUBERCULATED.—Marked with tubercles.

TUBERCULOUS.—Shaped like a tubercle.

TUMID.—Swollen, enlarged, inflated.

TURBINATED.—Top-shaped.

TURRETTED.—Shaped like a tower.

ULATE }
ULIFORM } .—Awl-shaped.

UMBILICATED.—Provided with an umbilicus.

UNGUIFORM.—Nail-shaped.

VENTRICOSE.—Swollen.

VITREOUS.—Glassy.

WORKS ON THE MICROSCOPE.

——oo——

In Crown 8vo, Cloth, with 38 Illustrations, on hot-pressed paper, price 2s. 6d.; in half Morocco, Roxburgh style, 4s. 6d.

THE STUDENT'S HANDBOOK
TO THE MICROSCOPE.

A PRACTICAL GUIDE TO ITS SELECTION AND MANAGEMENT.

By A QUEKETT CLUB-MAN.

Author of " My Microscope, and Some Objects from My Cabinet."

"Will speak for itself, and will prove an immense boon to beginners, who cannot be too strongly urged to provide themselves with it from the outset. Nowhere else is there to be found in such a convenient compass the special kind of information they need. . . Worthy of the attention of advanced miscroscopists."—*Literary World.*

"Written by a practical man, solely in the interests of students of microscopy, we would recommend the perusal of the book to every tyro."—*Schoolmaster.*

"No better guide, combined with cheapness of price, has ever yet been published."—*Naturalists' Monthly.*

"It is the very book the young beginner wants."—*Science Gossip.*

"Affords much practical information."—*Bookseller.*

"This exceedingly useful manual."—*Naturalists' Monthly.*

"Sure to be acceptable to a very numerous class.—*Public Opinion.*

London :
ROPER & DROWLEY,
29, LUDGATE HILL, E.C.

www.ingramcontent.com/pod-product-compliance
Lightning Source LLC
Chambersburg PA
CBHW031345020726
47499CB00005B/1407